INK DROPS 1

CREATIVE WRITINGS FROM GLOBAL VOICES

Edited by

WILLIAM GENSBURGER

Inkdrops I: Creative Writings from Global Voices

Edited by William Gensburger

Print ISBN: 979-8-9933226-4-3

CONTENTS

INK DROPS 1: Creative Writings from Global Voices

Edited by William Gensburger

Published by B&P Books

©2025 B&P Books, LLC

Print ISBN:

www.BNPBooks.com

FOREWORD

From my early recollection, I've always been enamored by good short stories. Unlike a novel, a short story has to grab you relatively quickly and hold you for the duration. It's not an easy feat, and not everybody can do that.

In this first anthology from Books and Pieces Magazine, we feature 12 stories that I believe you'll enjoy. Well, 10 stories, one novella, and a story of my own. Writers come from across the planet.

It is my hope that we'll publish two anthologies each year featuring the best stories that we receive.

I appreciate your support of indie authors (who do get a royalty share from this publication) and of the ongoing support for Books & Pieces Magazine, B&P Books, and of course, our BNPBookshop.

Enjoy this collection.

Regards,

William Gensburger
Author/Publisher

1

THE PRICE OF A SNEAK-PEAK, A STORY BY RATHIN BHATTACHARJEE

"Remember, my Boy, you shouldn't be too inquisitive for this nature of yours might land you in serious trouble, keeping you away from making friends, especially with the opposite sex." The voice in my head told me this one bleak afternoon. But despite the warning of the Voice, I did make friends with the first stunner in my life when I was still more of a shy youth. It happened when my nephew and I were playing cricket on the terrace of our house one fading afternoon.

Ours was a big house with some twenty-six rooms, stretching in all directions from North to South and West to East. Though my Baba and his brothers had separate kitchens each, by the time we grew up, the remnants of the joint family system still prevailed in our household.

I was always the batter as I liked hitting out. My nephew Tapan whom I fondly called Tapu, on the other hand, didn't mind bowling for hours. He wanted to be a first bowler like Denice Lilee.

We had stood a piri for the wickets and he was bowling real quick from a distance of some fifteen feet. I don't remember if he was bowling underarm. The next ball came charging like a tornado at me. I swung my bat at it with all my might, more out of fear than anything else. The ball hit a nearby wall on the right before ricocheting off it into the narrow galli between our house and the next on the western side. Tapu immediately ran down the steps in the west wing of the house while I, the more lethargic of the two, climbed up the stiff wall on the left leading to the dried up water tank in a corner above the open staircase.

I must have gotten silently into the tank before looking down at the narrow, garbage-filled up, untraded galli. I wouldn't deny that I was unaware of the bathroom down at the south-east end of the other house but what never came to my silly head was that when there was a bathroom, it was meant to be used by people. Real people of flesh and blood.

I had hardly turned my head from the heaps of rubbish that lay scattered all over the galli past the ghostly kitchen window of the other house, up the wall when a movement inside the bathroom below caught my attention. I must have been a little more than sixteen at that time.

There was a girl taking a shower in the bathroom, who couldn't have been much older than me. She, I guessed, was the daughter of the house owner and had recently returned from the UK or somewhere else. Naturally, the skin of the lady was translucent, glowing in the fading sun.

With her shapely figure and black curly hair, she struck me as the most gorgeous thing on two legs I had seen till then in my life. Women are said to have the sixth instinct. Hypnotized, I crouched inside the tank, my eyes level with the edge of the wall of the triangular tank, unable to look away from her bathing act when, turning her head, she looked up straight at me. Though my eyes were not even an inch above the wall, she must have sensed my presence from my protruding head.

"Wai! You rascal. What are you doing up there sneak-peeking into my bathroom....?" She was livid. She had somehow covered the lower part of her body with an outstretched hand while, with her back to me, she was trying to turn the shower off with her other hand. She looked even more breathtaking with the water dripping off her body.

I had rarely been that scared! The voice was yelling in my head constantly to find out ways of saving myself. Turning towards the open end of the galli, I cried out :

"Tapu. The ball is down there, behind those fungus-covered bricks? Can't you see it, you blockhead?"

The truth was Tapu was nowhere to be seen! I kept on talking to the imaginary Tapu for some more, praying all the while that no one came out of one of the adjacent buildings up to the galli, wondering who I thought I was talking to when there was not a soul to be seen in the vicinity!

"So, you've finally got it? No, no, don't throw it up. I'm coming down instead. Time to stop our game, OK? You'll be the one to bat first tomorrow, I promise." I kept speaking to the imaginary nephew while it was an effort not to look behind to appraise the graceful beauty one last time. My entire being though was crying out all through to God to save me from the pathetic plight.

Surprisingly, she didn't harangue me any more. Possibly, she had fallen for my ploy. But if I thought that that was the end of my woe, I was much mistaken. That evening, standing in the veranda of our house, located centrally above the entrance, I happened to see her again in the room on my left. The chink between the curtains let me have enough space to steal a look at her. She was practising, sitting like Goddess Saraswati behind a guitar. Her sweet voice mesmerized me and I stood there rooted, listening to her.

She couldn't have noticed me. I would have continued standing there had her brother not turned up just then. Tiptoeing from behind, he blindfolded her with his hands to my utter dismay. To my dismay because I didn't like his presence a wee bit as I wanted to be there in that room talking to her, teasing and praising her, trying to impress and make friends with her at the same time.

If you want something from the bottom of your heart, all elements in nature are believed to conspire together to fulfill your wishes. I read it somewhere. It was at around seven thirty in the evening when my cousin called me from her room on the second floor.

"Raj Da, are you coming up? All my friends are here, along with the relatives. It's time to cut the cake, you know." She said with the pang of discontent in her voice.

I remembered just then that it was her birthday. I had already bought a book for her as she was a bookworm.

"Yea, yea. I'll be there in a minute.."

"Come fast. I want to introduce you to Mitadi, our next door neighbour, you know." She blurted out hurriedly and got inside.

I got into a T-shirt over the faded jeans and scurried up to the spacious room of my uncle.

The first person that caught my attention as soon as I stepped into the room was that stunning lady. She had a dark green, cashmere pullover on, open at the neck that showed her collar bones prominently with the gold chain around the V of her neck. In the tight-fitting, black jeans, she looked fabulous and for reasons not clear to me at that time, I found it hard to take my eyes off her.

"Raj da, come here. Let me introduce Mita Di to you. She's just back from the USA…" Then turning to my tormentor on her right, she exclaimed," Mita Di, this is Raj, my cousin I was talking to you about. Isn't he the most handsome bloke around?"

I had my head down until I heard her chuckling. "So, you're the monarch of everything you survey here? (Raj, roughly translated in Bengali, would mean something like that!) Look at you blushing, Boy," she spoke with a cutting edge in her voice.

I looked into her eyes then. God! Her emerald eyes kept taunting and tormenting me. I would have kept looking at that hypnotic pair of eyes even then, oblivious of everything else around me if someone had not come rushing in our direction just then.

"There you're, Mitu! Transformed into a glam doll. I'll have to get you hooked on to someone before you leave the party tonight." It was Gita Aunty, the sole purpose of whose life was match-making, I mean, finding grooms for unmarried daughters of marriageable age.

"Mitu, I was told that you are a very adept singer. Why don't you sing a few English numbers for us? Anything of your choice, just to keep us entertained." As Gita Aunty kept pestering her for a song, I slowly retreated to the door.

"I'll if there are no lecherous eyes feasting on me here as well." To me, she sounded far from kidding.

Before anyone could make out what she was speaking about, I was out of the room. Feeling very lonely then, I climbed up the wooden staircase to the roof of the house.

There were not too many skyscrapers in our locality in Central Calcutta in those days. The shadowy Howrah Bridge looked downcast unlike the silver ball up in the sky. Though my mind was in a turmoil, everything around me looked serene and subdued.

I must have been sitting there for some time when I heard someone coming up the stairs. Next moment, she was there standing in front of me. There was something about this full moon night that made you a lunatic. Soon, we were chatting like long-lost friends. I asked her how long she intended to stay in Calcutta, whether she liked Calcutta more or New Jersey, if she missed India, and all that, while she asked me what I was planning to do after High school.

Soon, she was asking me if I had a girlfriend, and when I shook my head, she sighed stating that things in India were quite different from what they were in the USA. That's why the boys here looked famished.

I nearly jumped out of my skin when she asked me if I

had ever kissed a girl in my life and if not, how unfortunate I was. Now, if I am projecting the picture of a very cheap lady in your eyes, dear reader, please forgive me my writing skills. For she was anything but cheap. She was a very friendly, frank lady that I had the pleasure of setting my eyes early on in life.

I don't know when or how we came quite close to one another but when we did, I could smell her refreshing perfume that started wreaking havoc in me, stirring something long asleep up in me.

"You know, Raj, I was mad at you this afternoon. I wanted to come and complain to Dev Uncle straight away about your prying nature. But then, luckily for us, I realised my mistake. Residing in The States, I have forgotten most of what constitutes Indian culture and customs. Later, when I saw you again, standing in the veranda, you looked so lost and love-lorn that I felt sorry for you. The idea of coming and attending the birthday bash materialised in my head then. You know, you look even more dashing from close quarters." She stopped then with her mouth curved into a Monalisa-like smile, inches away from mine.

"I know, you'll forget me with the passage of time taking it as a fling. But you'll always remember me as the girl …." her voice sounded far off and husky at that time." I'll make sure that you remember me as the girl who kissed you first in your life." She sighed dreamily.

The next moment was surreal. She touched my lips with hers lightly at first as I could feel her eyes on me. Then the fairies started spreading their wings as I could taste the sweetness on the tip of my tongue and lip. I pulled her towards me, desperate to take her in my arms. She must have sensed my hunger as she, looking divine, came willingly into mine, as if ready to surrender herself to the demands of a sixteen-year-old.

That was the night the man took hold of me, having replaced the sixteen-year-old for good. That was also the night when, under the spent moon, Mita, with tears welling up in her eyes and the most heavenly smile on her lips, asked me to always call her by her first name, Mita, meaning friend.//

ABOUT THE AUTHOR

Rathin Bhattacharjee from Kolkata, India, graduated from C.U.

He joined BCSC as an English Teacher in 1990. Awarded His Majesty's Gold Medal (2018) for Lifetime Achievement in Teaching, he has been published and anthologised in a host of Indian and international magazines.

His novel, "The Damon in Doctor's Disguise" on Web Novel and 4 more books, all published by Zorbabooks, have won critical acclaim. His latest book entitled "'I Love You' in the ICU & 20 Other Stories" was released recently.

He loves writing, blogging, translating, podcasting, critiquing, and editing.

https://www.facebook.com/rathin.bhattacharjee.1

COMING SOON

BOOKS AND PIECES MAGAZINE and B&P BOOKS will be offering a comprehensive short story course talk by best-selling author JC Ryan and William Gensburger, best-selling author and publisher.

THE FOUR-WEEK online course will cover all aspects of short story writing from conception to submission with intensive lessons, Q&A sessions with both authors, multiple handouts, and a certificate of completion.

THIS COURSE IS DESIGNED for writers who wish to improve their skills, as well as new writers wishing to learn. Learn more at <u>www.BNPMag.com</u> and sign up for our early bird discount.

I ASK MY WIFE WHAT I SHOULD WRITE ABOUT AND SHE SAYS, "SEED PODS" AND OTHER POEMS BY JOHN BRANTINGHAM & SHAYMAA MAHMOUD

I Ask My Wife What I Should Write About and She Says, "Seed Pods"

I think about seed pods tonight,
those buried under the snow,

all that potential energy hidden

the way wasp larvae
are buried in fruit
the way the Andromeda Galaxy

the whole damn thing
gets hidden by the sun
because the sun reveals

that which is on earth
but hides all the rest of it,
and you are on earth

and not awake yet
because I'm always the one
with insomnia, so I spend

half of most nights reading
except that's not what
I'm doing tonight.

Tonight, I'm writing
this poem to you.

Merely Transformed

I still can't think of figs the same way,

Knowing a wasp crawls inside to die,
To make the fruit we call ambrosia,
Smash by the bushel into crimson jam.

The way a dandelion whittles itself down
Like shimmered milkweed fluff floating
Off, making new weeds a mile, twenty away,
offering flowers to bees after the harsh winter.

The way life works, casts a shadow:
The thrumming of negative space
Between the light and the rest
Like a death doula, a weeping willow.

The things that we lose making us
Whole in some other way, and all
We have to do is buy them the time to
Show us what's just on the other side.

Coming Across The Ice

This year Lake Erie
froze over.
I could trudge
my way across
and into Canada
if I wanted,
walk across water

like an Old Testament
prophet, walk
across like a man
fleeing his past,
walk across this lake
which is really a sea,
walk out to the middle
so far out
that the earth's
curve would hide
even the notion
of land. I stare
and dream of that
from the pier
with the dog as you
are inside the place
buying fish and chips.
I can hear the lonely
wind blowing
across the ice.
It kicks up dust devils
filled with snow
instead of dust
that the dog barks at.
I imagine she
hates how lonely
they seem.

ABOUT THE POETS

. . .

John Brantingham is currently and always thinking about radical wonder. He is a New York State Council on the Arts Grant Recipient for 2024, and he was Sequoia and Kings Canyon National Parks' first poet laureate. His work has been in hundreds of magazines and The Best Small Fictions 2016 and 2022. He has twenty-two books of poetry, nonfiction, and fiction.

Shaymaa Mahmoud has a Master's in International Relations with a Historical Perspective from Leiden University, and double Bachelors in English and Gender & Women's Studies from UC Berkeley. As an activist, writer and travel and nature enthusiast, she is committed to advocacy, reparative justice and decolonization. She was the Poetry Editor for Rind Literary Magazine for several years and has been published in places like The Chiron Review, CLAM, Village Poets Anthology and East Jasmine Review. She is working on two flash fiction novels and lives in New York, drawing out plans for a tiny house and trying to fill it with the witchiest stuff she can find.

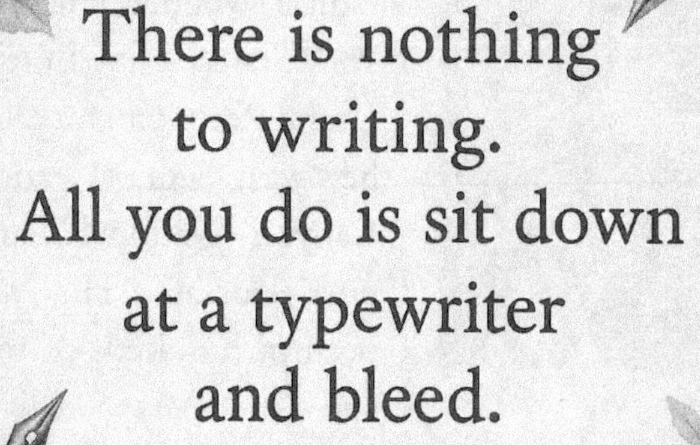

There is nothing
to writing.
All you do is sit down
at a typewriter
and bleed.

– Ernest Hemingway

THE COLD EMBRACE OF WINTER.
A STORY BY HUMA FATIMA

"This world is a cold place, be it winters or summers, my son. If only I could fill it with a little love and little warmth for you," she had once told me.

I would smile at her and say, "But I love winters, Mama. And I can always wear a jacket for warmth."

Throughout my childhood, I recalled how she laughed at my innocent comment. But now that I remember vividly, I cannot deny that a tear had rolled down her blushing cheek and she had smiled even when her heart was weeping.

I can't help but cry as they relentlessly push against the door, causing panic to surge through me. Later, when I regain composure, I'll look back and surely laugh at my helplessness. But for now, I'm immobilized, unable to muster the strength to flee.

Each thud against the door seems to amplify the impending threat of danger. Their words, "Open up, don't play smart. You are under arrest," echo through the door, sending shivers down my spine.

My gang loves my passionless stance, calling me the best bandit, but they forgot to tell me that in situations like these, I will die alone. Fear, a sensation never before felt this strongly, surges through my veins, and my breath is shallow and rapid.

"Not so soon," I mutter, forcing my legs to move. I grab the gun, its cold metal biting into my skin and leap towards the window. My pulse drowns out the chaos outside as I fumble for my mobile, scrolling through contacts with trembling fingers. The adrenaline makes my breath quicken, and my hands shake uncontrollably.

"The number you have dialed is not answering." The automated voice seems like a cruel joke, mocking my desperation. I try another number, then another. Each unanswered call feels like a punch in the gut, deepening my sense of isolation.

All my life, I was told that I was loved, and even though I sensed their deceit, it never bothered me. I always thought I could handle it, that I could play the game as well as they did. But it does trouble me today, as I now see the betrayal behind their elaborate promises. The friends I once trusted, and the loyalty I held onto, all vanish in this moment of need. My heart thumps as I dial yet another number, wishing deeply for someone to respond.

The window beckons like a last chance at freedom. I calculate the drop, knowing I must jump before it's too late. Yet, my feet feel rooted to the ground, weighed down by my mistakes and regrets. I swallow hard, fighting back tears that blur my vision. I've always been skilled at running away, but now fear holds me tight, reminding me of the deep solitude I find myself in.

"You know why I feel sorry for you?" Gunda Dada had asked me on the day it rained and the day I lost her.

"Because my mother is dead," I replied.

"No, it is because I plan to make you a prosperous man, but I am going to take from you one thing that you will regret giving me when you grow up." His words echo in my mind as unwanted tears fill my eyes, bringing back forbidden memories.

Tears are like uninvited guests, appearing unexpectedly on random days

Tears are like uninvited guests, appearing unexpectedly on random days. They can come suddenly, not just during sorrow but also in moments of confusion, joy, or nostalgia, catching you off guard while you go about your day. A surge of emotions can surprise you while doing simple tasks like gazing out the window or washing dishes. In those moments, tears may flow, bringing forth hidden feelings that have been waiting to emerge. You may try to blink them away, but they often persist, refusing to depart until they have made you feel something you weren't ready to face.

I had killed Uncle Asher at the age of thirteen, on what must have been the same day he murdered my mother. I recall how my hands shook as I gripped the rifle, my pulse racing with dread and wrath. I fired four shots at him, each fueled by a distinct, horrible memory.

The first shot was for not dying with my father when he perished in that road accident. He had always claimed to be my father's closest friend, but a true friend would not have survived while his brother-in-arms was taken away so brutally. The second bullet was for having the guts to ask for my mother's hand in marriage while giving her barely enough time to grieve. The third shot rang out as he placed his hands around her throat, the rage in his eyes as bright as the rising sun, punishing her for rejecting his twisted proposal. The fourth and final shot was for killing her while I watched from behind the curtain, too afraid to move, too small to comprehend but old enough to feel the weight of the horror unfolding in front of me.

Even his angels, if he had any, would not know that I had seen everything. That I had borne witness to the monster he truly was. By the time he had stopped breathing, I would too become a monster, with the gun that my Dada had trusted me with and a promise of always staying loyal to it.

The door's band comes out with a rattle, and to my surprise, it is not the officers who enter.

"Ouch." I feel the bullet penetrating my body, and I yelp in absolute pain.

"A criminal never dies at the hands of law; he dies at

the hands of his men when he tries to deceive them." A familiar voice hit my ears, and I caught Dada standing at a distance, deeply enjoying my shrieks and suffering.

In a rare moment of bravery, I grab my gun and shoot at him, and they fire at me in return. One way or another, the gun is an object that belongs to me. The only thing I remember, which was never meant for me, is happiness; it is something I regret giving away.

The last thing I hear is a whisper from my flinching Dada.

"You shouldn't have reported me, son." He gives out a loud chuckle, forgetting for one trivial moment that blood is furiously shooting out from his wound and life is draining out of him gradually.

As the stars shine brighter, darkness descends on me like heavy winter snow. I lie there, recalling the soft melodies my mother sang. She seems to be calling me up to the stars, where I believe all the departed go. I forgot to ask her which star she lives on, and it troubles me to lose the address of my destination. But I reassure myself, "It's all right". I have already spent a lifetime looking up at the stars; I don't mind spending another waiting for her until she can see me and assure me that this one moment of my life is not a dream.

As my mother reaches for my hand and pulls me into her arms, a final thought crosses my mind: it didn't have to end this way. If I had chosen differently, I might have found warmth beyond this cold world, a place where love was not fleeting, and her voice was not a distant memory. I could have lived in a world where even her absence wouldn't make me a bad boy.

ABOUT THE AUTHOR

Huma Fatima is a 22-year-old writer from Pakistan, currently pursuing a degree in Computer Science. Although her academic background is rooted in technology, she has long been drawn to the art of storytelling.

Writing offers her a creative outlet beyond the boundaries of her technical studies, allowing her to explore human emotions, imagined worlds, and meaningful ideas. It is through writing that she expresses her voice most authentically, and she continues to develop her craft with dedication and purpose.

AND THEN THERE WAS ONE. A STORY BY E.P. LANDE

Adam looked at his caller ID. As he didn't recognize the number, he let it ring. A moment later, his iPhone rang a second time. This time he answered it.

"Is this Adam Herz?" the caller asked, "… the real Adam Herz?" Thinking the caller was a joker, but being somewhat amused, Adam said,

"Yes … but who are you?"

"John Newman. You may not remember but we were in the same cabin at Camp Wannatoo in 1952," the caller explained. Adam remembered being at that camp, seventy years before, but couldn't recall someone in the cabin by that name.

"I took a photo of our group and would like to send it to you, — that is, if you want it," the caller offered. "Do you want the photo?" the caller asked.

"Sure," Adam said, "… send it."

A moment later, Adam received an email from John Newman and attached was the photo of a group of young boys in front of a cabin, and another attachment that read as though it were part of a newsletter. Sitting in the front row, Adam recognized himself. He called John Newman.

"Thanks for the photo," he said. "I recognize myself. Who are the others?"

"Standing in the back are Tommy. Next to Tommy is Irwin, then Eddie, and next to Eddie is Bobby. Sitting in front are Gregg, you, and Billy. I'm not in the picture as I took it," John explained.

"I remember some of the names but not the faces," Adam said. "Where are they all now?"

"Dead; they're all dead," John told him. "You and I are the only ones still alive."

On hearing this, Adam was a little disturbed by the blunt manner in which John Newman conveyed the news. But then, realizing that his cabinmates of seventy years before would have been, like himself, over 80, that they were all dead was perhaps natural.

"When did they die?" Adam was fascinated that out of

the eight boys in his cabin, only John Newman and he were still around.

"It's a long story — actually, six long stories," John said. "Why don't we meet? I remained in touch with each of them, so I can fill you in on the details. Where have you spent your life?"

"Soon after I graduated from university, my late wife and I moved to France. When she died, I decided to spend the rest of what was remaining of my life here, in Vermont."

"Well, let's you and I get together."

"When do you want to meet?" Adam asked … hesitating … but he was intrigued.

"Well, how about next week? I spend my summers at my cabin on the Maine coast. Why don't you drive over and spend a few days? We can catch up."

"Sure; send me your address. I could come next Monday."

After he hung up, Adam sat back in his chair, looking at the photo John had emailed and mused about his cabin-mates of seventy years before. Was Tommy the swimmer? Or had it been Gregg? Irwin had been a baseball player, he recalled. Who had been good at archery? Eddie? One of the boys had been an adventurer, reading up on caves in the area, always trying to find ones that no one had ever discovered. And then there was …. He looked at the photo closely. One of them had been associated with the theatre; the camp put on plays every summer. Was it … yes, John himself. Adam looked, but couldn't really attach an activity to their faces.

During his drive to Maine, Adam continued thinking

about his cabinmates. He seemed to recall that John had been the camp track star. He wondered what John looked like now. Had he kept in shape over the years? Adam looked forward to hearing John tell him stories associated with each of the boys. As Adam's days were more or less free now, his visit would be like reading a good book — or perhaps he could turn it into a decent book.

Where John lived was quite isolated and rather barren, Adam thought as he pulled up to the house. The cabin sat almost at the edge of a cliff with a view of the Maine coast-line that was breathtakingly dramatic.

"You found me," John exclaimed. "Here, let me help you," and took Adam's overnight case. Adam followed John into the cabin and out onto the porch.

"Your view is quite spectacular," Adam remarked, looking at the ocean perhaps a couple of hundred feet below the cliffs

"It's my sanctuary," John replied. "I stay here from May until October, and often take long weekends from time to time during the other months, just to relax. Will you join me for some chardonnay?"

Adam watched John as he left to fetch the wine. He still couldn't remember him from their summers at Camp Wannatoo. But seeing him was a bit of a shock. While they were more or less the same age, to Adam, John looked a good twenty years older. He walked stooped, with a slight hesitation. As the camp's track and field star, Adam had expected John to have retained a somewhat solid build, but he was scrawny. What was left of his all-white hair, he wore closely cropped, and though he sported a tan, his complexion was splotchy. John had on a flannel shirt, open at the collar, but missing a couple of buttons, and his grey flannel slacks were stained in places. Instead of shoes or loafers, he wore a pair of well-worn slippers.

"Here you go," John said as he handed Adam a glass of wine. "To us — the remaining two — and to memories of Camp Wannatoo."

They sat, chatting about camp. Adam was intrigued by John's enthusiasm about his experiences at the camp over the summers.

"For me, it opened up a new world," John said.

"What do you mean?" Adam asked, then added, "I never really liked camp. Living in a cabin, eating camp food, and scheduled activities. None of that was for me. I told my parents they were wasting their money, that I would be happier simply staying home …."

"Doing what? At camp, I picked up that you weren't a joiner, Adam."

"I preferred to do things by myself — and I still do. But you said that camp …."

"It gave me the opportunity to explore the world around me as well as my inner being," finishing Adam's question. "It was the theatre."

"Now I recall that you were always quoting stuff none of us had ever heard of."

"I was rehearsing the lines of the play I would be acting in. You remember, the camp put on one, sometimes two plays every summer, and I made sure I was in each one. But let's have dinner, shall we?" Adam followed John to the dining room table.

The cabin consisted of three rooms — the two bedrooms and a central room, part of which was the living space, part, the kitchen, and next to the kitchen, John's dining room table made of a single hand-sawed wood plank that resembled maple, its pedestal being the root of a dead — but cured — apple tree, John told Adam.

"You must have read about Irwin; it was all over the news," John told Adam during dinner. "Suicide," John said, as he cleared the salad plates.

"I remember something about it in the International Herald Tribune. I read the paper religiously when I lived in France, as it was my primary source of news from home," Adam told him.

"Irwin was a complicated person," John said when he returned from the kitchen with the roast chicken. "I can still hear him boasting to all of us in the cabin, about the car his father drove — as if a car was something to be proud of."

"Yeah, he was always telling us that what he — or someone in his family — had was better or worth more than anything any of us had," Adam said. "It got to be annoying. The chicken is excellent, John. But tell me, how did he commit suicide? I don't recall that part in the article in the Tribune."

"We would visit each other from time to time. On my last visit to his place, he began telling me how he regretted all his boasting; Irwin had always been a braggard, even after we left Camp Wannatoo. We were sitting in his living room when he began sobbing and asking me to forgive him."

"Why would he do that?"

"I guess he thought of me as a close friend. As I said, we would see one another, as old friends do, but I never confided in him, and I always thought that whatever he told me was a stretch from the truth. I would read his daily postings on Instagram and Facebook and laugh; I knew they were far from his reality, but that was Irwin."

"I don't believe in social media, so I never read any of his postings," Adam said. "I hope you'll share your recipe for this chicken; it's simply the best I've ever eaten." John cut Adam a wing and a leg and placed both on Adam's plate.

"From his postings, the world must have thought Irwin to be the most generous, loving, considerate, and charming individual on this planet," John continued. "But I knew better. You know, he had to leave the University of Pennsylvania for plagiarism, and his first wife took him to court for nonpayment of child support? Do you like the wine?" John asked, pouring Adam another glass.

"From what I remember of Irwin at camp, he wasn't all that smart, and definitely not generous," Adam recalled. "He would never share any of the packages of candy he received from home, unlike the rest of us."

"As I was telling you, he invited me to his home, principally to absolve himself of his boastings over the years. I felt I was being asked to act as his father confessor." John sat back in his chair and watched as Adam sipped the wine. "Irwin also liked his wine — and his whiskey, too. I think that all his boasting caused him to drink."

"What do you mean?" Adam asked, placing his glass of wine on the table.

"Drinking, to Irwin, was his penitence. He drowned his boastful pride so that he didn't have to hear himself. Over the years, he became an alcoholic. He married several times, and each wife divorced him. His children would have nothing to do with him. I was probably the only friend he had left."

"He must have been miserable," Adam said.

"He was, and that was probably the reason for him to commit suicide. I knew that he took morphine …."

"Morphine? That's a pretty powerful drug."

"He told me sometime earlier that he needed to take a small dose to sleep. To me, he took it to forget. The last night I was with him, we had a couple of drinks with our meal and afterward he told me he just wanted to get some sleep. I said goodnight. That was the last time I saw him alive. The following morning, when I got up and went to his room, I found him sprawled across his bed, an open bottle of morphine pills on his night table next to a glass of water. I called an ambulance immediately. The doctor in the ER at the hospital pronounced him dead, and an autopsy confirmed my suspicion that he had overdosed on the morphine."

"I'm driving to your place for the weekend," John texted Irwin.

"Great. I'll stock my wine cellar and have plenty of booze on hand," Irwin texted back. Afterward, Irwin speculated about John's reason for his visit. It was true that over the years they had been accustomed to see one another, but somehow John's text seemed rather strange, abrupt; he wondered what his friend wanted.

"Glad you stocked up," were John's first words when they greeted one another on his arrival.

"I had Sherry-Lehmann ship me a case of Kistler Chardonnay, and I have the Macallan triple cask 15-year-old Scotch you always drink. They were out of the 18-year-old," Irwin told his friend.

"Let's have a starter, shall we?' John suggested as they walked into Irwin's home.

"Excuse the clutter," Irwin said. "My housekeeper didn't come in this week; family emergency. Neat?" he asked.

"One rock; it's the first …."

"Since breakfast," Irwin added, mirthfully.

"Okay, since breakfast. Anyway, you know I always have it on one rock before noon."

Soon the two friends were drinking the Kistler Chardonnay, John having had three shots of the Macallan, Irwin nursing his first, to which he had added a fistful of ice.

"What brings you here?" Irwin asked, refilling John's wine.

"Nothing special. I needed a first-hand fix of telling you about my life. Instagram isn't the same as hearing it directly from my mouth," John laughed.

Irwin smiled, for he knew his friend. He himself liked to boast, but John's Instagram postings gave pride a bad reputation. They spent the remainder of the afternoon bragging, John recounting about his investments — double-digit returns on the stocks he purchased; about his travels — he recently returned from fishing in Bariloche, where he landed the largest fish ever caught in Argentinian waters; about his art collection — he just bought the finest Fauve Derain. Irwin told John about the latest addition to his rare automobiles — the Lamborghini SC18 Alston he picked up for a 'song'; the George 1 flatware service for 12 with the king's monogram — until Irwin told John he needed some sleep.

"Can you let me have a few of your morphine pills?" John asked? "I think I need one. I'm all hyped up."

"Help yourself. They're in the medicine cabinet in my bathroom," Irwin told him.

"Let's have a nightcap," John said when he returned to where they were having their drinks. He went into the kitchen and brought back two glasses of Macallan, handing one to Irwin.

"Here's to us," John said and drank his shot. "Drink up, my friend." He watched as Irwin tilted his head back and drank.

"Wow, this stuff is strong," Irwin said. "I feel woozy, like I've had a few …." He didn't finish. He tried to rise but sat back down. "What did you give me?" he asked, his head in his hands.

"You just had 250 milligrams of morphine," John told him.

"Whaaat?" Irwin slurred.

"You heard me. I've had enough of your bullshit. All you ever do is talk about yourself, filling your fuckin' Instagram postings with garbage. Boasting is a sin that is rooted in pride."

Irwin slumped in his chair, unconscious. John dragged him to his bedroom, undressed him and placed him sprawled across the bed. He brought Irwin's glass and placed it with the now-empty container of morphine pills on the bed beside him, wiping them both clean of his own fingerprints. He then left the room, shut the door, and walked into his own bedroom and went to sleep.

"I'm not sure I'll be able to sleep after what you just told me," Adam said. "My heart is pounding in my chest. But I'll not ask you for morphine. Good night, John."

The following day, after breakfast, John suggested they take a walk.

"I still can't get over what you told me yesterday about Irwin," Adam said as they were walking along the cliff on which John's cabin was built. "It kept me awake."

Stopping, John said, "Adam, Irwin was a drunk and wallowed in self-pity. It was a coincidence that I happened to be there when he did it, otherwise, I, too, would have found out by reading about it in the New York Times." They continued walking in silence.

"Ed — do you remember him?" John asked. "Ed left camp early one summer."

"I vaguely remember. Something about his grandfather."

"Ed's grandfather had become rich lending money to recent immigrants," John began, "charging them exorbitant interest …."

"Are you saying his grandfather was a loan shark?"

"Ed wouldn't have called him that, but that's what his grandfather was. One of his clients couldn't pay. Ed's grandfather had his men threaten the guy — you know, break his legs, that sort of thing. I guess the immigrant lost it. He walked into the office when he knew Ed's grandfather would most likely be alone and killed him." John said this is such a matter-of-fact tone that Adam thought he hadn't understood what John was telling him.

"Ed's parents took him out of Wannatoo. I didn't hear from him until a few years later," John continued. "We had both graduated from university by then. He invited me to have lunch with him. During our lunch, Ed told me how he had taken over his grandfather's business and was now making so much money he didn't know how to spend or invest it — other than by expanding his moneylending, but some of the immigrants had made a little and were lending to one another, cutting in on his turf, as he put it. When I told him about a pasta company I was considering to buy, he offered to help me.

"I borrowed the money … reluctantly. I didn't really need it, but he insisted, almost throwing it at me. I knew Ed was somewhat of a sociopath, making money without thinking of the harm he was causing those who borrowed from him, but he was insistent." They stopped and admired the waves crashing against the jagged rocks below. "About six months later, Ed came here to visit. By this time, I had just about repaid the loan as the pasta company was doing phenomenal business.

"He probably came to thank me and ask if I had another deal that could use his financing. He said he was still making a fistful off of the immigrants, despite the competition. We were walking along the cliffs, like you and I are now. It was drizzling, making walking a little slippery. I told him to be careful, but Ed was so into telling me about the money he was making that he wasn't paying attention. He slipped …."

"You're not telling me he …."

"I'm afraid I am. I tried to grab him, but our hands were wet and I couldn't hold on. They found him, his head bashed in, on the rocks below."

"Ed, let's you and me get together and have lunch,"

John suggested in a text. "I have a business proposition I want to discuss with you."

"You say there's something you want to talk to me about?" Ed asked when he and John were having lunch the following day. "If I can make a buck, why not? That's my trade. What do you have in mind?"

"We both have done pretty damn well …."

"If I'm not for me, who will be? It's my motto," Ed said as he dug into his steak.

"You and I are the same, Ed. One never has enough. Before my parents died in that automobile accident, I made sure I was their sole executor. They trusted me, the poor bastards. Anyway, I'm thinking of buying US Pasta …."

"That's a big enterprise, John. Do you have the dough?"

"That's where you come in. I hope you'll lend me …."

"How much?" Ed asked.

"$5 million," John told him.

"You know my terms."

"Yeah, but I hope to make a lot on this deal, so I expect to repay you within a year."

Six months later, Ed called. "John, we need to talk. That loan you begged for, you haven't made any effort to repay. I'm coming to your cabin this afternoon."

"Ed, just give me more time," John asked when they were walking along the cliffs in front of John's cabin that afternoon. It had been raining but had stopped.

"You know the deal, John. I haven't made my fortune waiting to be repaid. Either repay the loan …."

"I'm not one of your immigrants, Ed," John told him. "No one but you and me knows about our arrangement. Without that loan hanging around my neck, I'll be able to make a hell of a lot more. What are you to me?" John moved closer to the edge, pulling Ed with him. "All you have is an insatiable desire to gain and hoard wealth," he told Ed … and let go.

Adam said he needed to return to the cabin, because what John had told him was causing him to feel dizzy. They walked back in silence. While Adam wasn't hungry, John insisted they eat something and suggested he make an omelette. John didn't appear to be disturbed in recounting the history of their friend's death while Adam ate without appetite.

"Gregg was a ball of fire," John said as he helped himself to another slice of the omelette. "Remember the socials the camp put on with the girls from Camp Andrascoggan?"

"Vaguely," Adam said, but his mind was still on what John had told him that morning.

"Gregg would spend the entire afternoon preparing. He went to the dances all dolled up," John mused. "He did the same afterward."

"What do you mean?" Adam asked, returning to the conversation.

"We attended the same university; pledged the same fraternity. We even shared a room together during our junior year. While I studied, Gregg talked about girls. It was like he had a perpetual hard-on. Lust, pure and simple. More omelette?" he offered.

"No thanks, but I will, a cappuccino," Adam told him. While John was making the cappuccinos, Adam tried to recall what Gregg looked like; all he could picture was a scrawny kid with hair growing out in every direction. Definitely not the sexy person John was describing.

"He got one of those diseases, the kind you get when you don't use condoms. I never met a hornier guy." John went to the kitchen and brought back some shortbread biscuits. "Have one," and handed Adam the plate. "But his appetite didn't stop at women. Gregg craved almost everything, but it was mostly his appetite for women that did him in."

"What do you mean?" Adam asked.

"He wanted to come here, he said to get away for a few days. I thought it would be fun, so I agreed. When he arrived, he had a woman with him. Given his history, I didn't say anything, but suggested — strongly — that the woman take his car and drive back to Boston, that I would bring Gregg with me as I had to return there that Monday. She agreed and left.

"We had a few drinks with lunch, and then Gregg announced that he wanted to take my kayak and tour the shoreline. I told him I didn't think it was a good idea as the kayak was to be used in the nearby lake, not in the ocean. But Gregg insisted. I watched as he carried the kayak to the cliffs and down the stone steps to the inlet below. That was the last I saw of him … until his body washed up the next morning."

"Gregg, this is John. Do you want to join me this weekend? The weather is beautiful. I guarantee you won't regret it … you know what I mean."

When Gregg arrived later that afternoon, he was greeted by a stunning woman wearing nothing but 6" red stilettos and a single strand of pearls.

"Hi," she said as she opened the door of Gregg's car and lifted him out into a bear hug, her ruby-red lips planted firmly on his.

"Nice to meet you, too," Gregg gasped when she released him.

"John said I should entertain you until he returns." She took Gregg by the arm and brought him into the cabin and straight to the guest bedroom, closing the door behind them.

Two hours later, when John returned from his shopping expedition in the village, the lady opened the bedroom door — still dressed in stilettos and the pearl necklace — walked to where John was standing, held out her hand into which John placed the keys to his suburban … and left.

"Did you have fun?" John smirked when Gregg — naked — emerged from the bedroom, looking a little bedraggled, staggering to the kitchen.

"That was one hot lady," Gregg managed to say between gulps of water.

"I told you you could expect a good time," John said. "I had her during the night, so I know exactly what you mean. Do you feel like taking the kayak for a spin?"

"I think I came three times," Gregg gasped. "It was amazing; I stayed hard the entire time. She's dynamite. I wish she'd stayed."

"When we go back to Boston, I'll ask her to join us. It won't be the first time you and I shared," John told him.

Gregg put on shorts and followed John along the cliffs and down the stone steps to where John left his kayak.

"Get in the bow," John instructed Gregg. "You don't look steady …."

"After what that lady put me through? You'd still be prostrate on your bed," and Gregg howled with laughter.

They pushed off, John paddling in the stern while Gregg spread his legs and basked in the sun. A couple of hundred yards off the shore, John rested his paddle on his thighs.

"A man who uses his body for lechery wrongs the Lord," he said.

"What are you talking about? Now you're sounding like a self-righteous minister," Gregg told him, still stretched out with his eyes closed. "Are you speaking about yourself?"

"When a person seeks sex for pleasure, he's sinning with lust." Saying this, John rose to his feet and, with the paddle, smacked Gregg on the side of his head. Then, rocking the kayak, tipped it over, sending Gregg into the swirling waters.

"What the fuck are you doing?" Gregg gasped when he surfaced.

John swam over to a flailing Gregg and, with force, pushed Gregg's head under the water and held it there until he felt no movement in Gregg's struggling body. He then dragged Gregg's lifeless body underneath the overturned kayak and swam to the shore.

"Would you like another cappuccino?" John asked.

"No thanks. If you don't mind, I might take a walk in your garden," Adam told him. What John had recounted about Gregg had shaken Adam. He wanted to be alone with his thoughts.

"Why don't we meet for drinks, say, around 5:00?" John suggested.

Strolling in the perennial garden, John's recounting

about Gregg and how he died hit Adam like a cold gust. He pulled his sweater closer around his body. Actually, thinking back to Camp Wannatoo, he thought Gregg was gay, but given what John had just told him, that must have been one of the other boys. He couldn't imagine anyone having such a strong sexual desire that it controlled his life — and, eventually, his death. Poor Gregg, — but then, he died a happy man, Adam imagined.

"What do you think of my roses?" John asked when they met for drinks later that afternoon.

"Beautiful, and somewhat unusual," Adam told him, "… especially the deep lavender ones."

"Yes, those I had a difficult time getting. Wine?" John asked.

"Red, please."

"There was this woman — a rose aficionado — who belonged to the same country club as I did. We would talk about gardens and flowers, and one day she invited me to visit her place. There I saw the deep lavender rose for the first time. I wanted it."

"Did she tell you where to buy a bush?"

"No, she changed the subject, but I pursued the issue, because I simply had to have it. I knew her husband was in a bit of a financial bind, so … I offered him a deal that I knew he wouldn't — couldn't — refuse … and part of my offer was the rose that you saw in my garden. Let's have dinner." Adam couldn't blame John for wanting the rose; it was unique.

"Shall I continue telling you about the others?" John asked. Adam understood he was referring to the boys in their cabin at camp, but after hearing him tell Adam how Irwin, Ed, and now Gregg, died, he wasn't as keen as he had been after he received his initial email, — but he was still curious.

"Remember, Billy?"

"Was he the camper who seemed envious every time one of us received a package from home?"

"Right. Billy received more packages than any of us, yet he was always there, right beside whoever was opening a parcel. It was as though he felt he should have been the one receiving the package. Talk about feeling entitled. More potatoes? As we lived in the same city, we would see each other occasionally — perhaps more than I saw the others — so I witnessed his behavior. He knew I collected hand-guns — some exceedingly rare — and asked if I would show him my collection. Shall we continue on the porch? I'll bring our coffees." Adam followed him and, while they drank their coffee, John continued.

"I agreed, and Billy confided in me that he, too, had started collecting handguns — to me, he was jealous of my collection — and was always looking for one that no one else owned. When he arrived at my home, he couldn't wait to see what I had. I felt he was too anxious. Some people collect Fabergé, some Impressionists, others, vintage wines; I collect rare handguns.

"I keep them in drawers in a vault in my basement, and only I know its combination. Billy's eyes were brighter than the evening stars and his hands trembled as I opened drawer after drawer. He asked if he could handle them. I was a little embarrassed by the manner in which he touched their surfaces, almost caressing them." John got up and walked to the edge of the porch, then turned.

"I hesitated before letting him handle the guns, as his hands were trembling, but he assured me that it was nothing but excitement. He was admiring my Colt 1849 pocket revolver, telling me he had never seen one like it — it's gold-inlaid — when my phone rang. I left him and went upstairs to answer it. As I was putting back the receiver, I heard a shot. I raced down to the vault, and there I saw Billy. He must have been fondling the Colt and it went off, hitting him in the forehead."

"Billy, come on down to my place this weekend. I bought a revolver at auction recently that I know you'll drool over," John suggested when he spoke to his friend.

Later, when they were talking in John's living room, "I noticed how you touched the Holland & Holland Royal Deluxe in my collection," Billy told John. "You were obviously so envious that I knew you would find one even rarer, just to be one up on me."

"I deserve to have the one I'm going to show you," John said.

"What is it?" Billy asked, becoming excited at the prospect of handling John's latest purchase.

"It's a Colt …."

"John, a Colt is a common handgun."

"Not this one. Come, I'll show it to you." John led Billy down the stairs to the basement vault where he kept his collection. Inside the vault, he opened a drawer and took out the handgun, handing it to Billy.

"Wow. This is beautiful. I wouldn't mind owning one like this," Billy said, caressing the gun's gold-inlaid handle.

"Check the barrel; it's as smooth as silk, the inside too," John told him. Billy raised the gun to eye level and peered into the interior of its barrel.

"Ever since we met at Camp Wanatoo, I felt you envied me," John said with contempt.

"This gun is amazing," Billy said, not listening to John.

"You've always felt entitled and deprived …."

"The interior of its barrel is as beautiful as its exterior," Billy said, closing his left eye and peering inside the barrel of the gun.

"I could never understand your reason for feeling someone — God? — owed you something …."

"What are you saying?" Billy asked, the barrel of the gun almost touching his eye.

"You know, Billy, envy is ugly and destructive …." and with one quick step, John was in front of Billy with both hands wrapped around Billy's hands that were holding the gun. John pulled the trigger. Billy fell to the ground.

"Where jealousy and selfish ambition exist, there will be disorder and every vile practice," he preached, looking at his dead friend. John then went upstairs and called 911.

"You didn't know it was loaded?" Adam asked.

"I had only recently purchased it at auction, so I assumed it wasn't."

Adam was shocked by what John had told him, but John continued to drink his wine, looking off in the distance. Adam felt his heart racing and started to have difficulty breathing. Since he arrived, John had told him that four of their cabinmates had died tragically, and there were still two more histories to recount. Adam began hoping that the two had died of heart attacks, even cancer would be more acceptable than how Irwin, Ed, Gregg, and Billy had met their ends.

"I think I'll take a nap," Adam told John.

"Do you take naps often?" John asked.

"I do, just not every day. This visit has been trying for me."

"If I remember, at camp you would go to our cabin after lunch while the rest of us played softball or went swimming. Did you nap then?" John's tone appeared to Adam to be judgmental, as though it were indolent to nap other than at night. Adam decided to ignore John's comment and went to his bedroom.

"How was your nap?" John asked as Adam came out of his bedroom two hours later. When Adam didn't reply, John asked,

"Shall I tell you about Tommy?"

"Can it wait 'til later?" Adam asked. "I need some time to fully take in what you told me about Billy."

"Okay, if that's the way you feel. We'll talk about Tommy over dinner."

While Adam really didn't feel like having John tell him of another tragic ending, he needed to close the book on the fates of Tommy and Bobby. "Why don't we walk along the cliffs? You can tell me while we stroll," Adam said.

"Tommy died in a truly tragic way," John said as they were walking. "If you remember, he loved food …."

"I recall he was always the first one in the dining room," Adam said, still not having fully recovered, but the breeze felt refreshing.

"Not only was he the first one, he piled his plate so

high he couldn't see over it when we all sat at the table to eat," John continued, smiling at the memory.

"We all thought it funny, at the time."

"But you see, Adam, it wasn't at all funny. It was gluttony, pure gluttony." John's voice had become deeper and he seemed, to Adam, to be making a point of what Adam didn't understand, then. In Adam's memory, John vied with Tommy for who could eat the most. They continued walking in silence, with only the water of the Atlantic slapping the boulders below.

"Over the years, I would see Tommy, usually for a dinner. He knew I owned a pasta company, and at one of our dinners, he asked if he might visit as he was curious to observe how pasta — real pasta — was made. So, I invited him.

"When he arrived, he immediately asked to visit the factory where he made a beeline for the machine into which we feed the pasta dough, extruding it in different widths, depending on the type of pasta we're making." As John told the story, Adam gazed out into the sea, admiring the seagulls flying.

"I was explaining to Tommy the steps by which dough is fed into the machine, when one of my workers called me away to ask a question. That's when it happened." As John said this, Adam turned and looked at his friend.

"What happened?" Adam asked, an uneasy feeling in his stomach.

"Tommy must have leaned over the machine and lost his balance ...."

"You're not saying ...."

"He lost his balance, and reaching for something with which to hold himself, his arm slipped in front of the grinder, pulling his body into the machine."

"John, I need to rest; the drive here was very tiring," Tommy said as he got out of his car in the parking lot of US Pasta, John's company. John had insisted that he visit the pasta factory that John had recently purchased.

"Come on, Tommy; you can rest after we visit the factory." As it was noon, all the workers were having their lunch in the factory's cafeteria.

"I wanna see how you make the dough," Tommy said as they entered John's factory.

"We'll see that later. Come, I want to show you the extruder. I think you'll enjoy watching the strands of pasta created from a mountain of dough," John told him.

As they stood in front of the extruding machine, John turned on the machine, then placed a hand firmly in the small of Tommy's back.

"Why are you pushing me?" Tommy asked.

"You're a fuckin' glutton, Tommy. You were always the first in line for dinner, and you ate like a pig." John's hand pushed Tommy closer to the machine. "I hate gluttons," and he pushed harder, until Tommy's body was bent over the extruding machine.

"Fuck, John, stop pushing me. I'll lose my balance."

"This is what gluttons like you deserve," and John pushed so hard that Tommy fell into the conveyor that was moving the dough into the grinder.

"John, stop …" were his last words as the claws of the grinder caught Tommy's arm and pulled his whole body into the machine.

"He must have died instantly. When I heard a scream, I turned, but there was nothing I could do. My foreman turned off the machine immediately, but it was too late. Tommy was pronounced dead by the nurse in our infirmary."

"What an awful way to die," Adam said, feeling nauseated by the image. "You must have been shaken — after all, it occurred in your factory."

"I can tell you, Adam, I was paralyzed. I closed the factory, of course. But let's talk about more pleasant things." They continued along the path back to the cabin, trying to make chitchat, but all Adam could think of was the vision of Tommy being sucked into the pasta grinder.

"Do you remember Bobby?" John asked as they were walking back to the cabin.

"Bobby? Was he the boy who always appeared to be angry?" Adam wondered.

"Bobby and I attended the same grammar school and high school in Philadelphia," John continued, "… so I had witnessed this kind of behavior before and after. Bobby was kicked out of our high school for trying to blackmail a teacher. It seems Bobby compromised this teacher, and when the teacher wouldn't give him an 'A' in some course, Bobby told him he'd tell the principal that the teacher had been sexually harassing him. The teacher hauled Bobby to the principal, who believed the teacher and expelled Bobby. In those days, people believed teachers and priests, not like today."

They returned to the cabin. Adam told John he needed to lie down. They decided to meet for dinner. Adam wasn't sure what it was, but, to him, John always seemed to be there when something happened. While what John just told him about Bobby could be true, he was having doubts. He decided to spend the night and leave in the morning.

"Bobby enjoyed exploring, especially caves," John told Adam while they were having drinks before dinner. "I'm not the adventurous type, but he insisted that I join him in France, to visit and explore some the caves in the Dordogne. I. knew not to refuse; agreeing to accompany him was, to me, easier than having him rage at me for not being there for him."

"Jeanne and I also visited caves in the Dordogne, as it wasn't a long drive from where we were living on the Côte d'Azur."

"A few years later, Bobby heard of some — to his way of thinking — really interesting caves in Thailand."

"Is that where the schoolboys and their leader got lost and had to be rescued?"

"Yes, and I was against it because of the risk, but Bobby persisted. When we arrived in Bangkok, the rains had stopped, so we set out for the first cave on Bobby's list, Mae Hong Son. Then, we visited the Phi Phi Islands, where there are cliffs — like mine — and clear coves. All was going well, and I didn't feel any tension or fear. Then Bobby insisted that we explore the Tham Luang Nang Non cave; it's between Thailand and Myanmar. I looked it up. I said I would go with him but would not enter the cave."

"Why?" Adam asked.

"It's over six miles long, with deep recesses, narrow tunnels, boulder chokes, collapses, and sumps. While I was fascinated by the stalagmites I'd seen in the Dordogne caves — and there were even more in the Tham Luang cave —

my interest stopped when I read about the dangers this cave presented, especially as we would be there in the off-season when guided tours had stopped. But that's what drove Bobby; he loved danger."

Adam listened, fearing what might come next. John appeared to be relaxed, as though he were telling Adam about his last golf game.

"We parked at the entrance to the cave. Its entrance is really out of this world — vast, high ceiling, many crevices. You could get lost just exploring the entrance. I told him I'd wait for him there, that he shouldn't stay exploring for more than a couple of hours. He'd checked where the master switch was for the lights that had been installed after school kids had been lost in 2018, and turned them on.

"While he explored, I sat and read a book I'd brought with me. After about an hour, I started to worry, but we had agreed that he could take a couple of hours, so I took up my book and tried to concentrate on reading. Suddenly, the lights went off; I wasn't left in total darkness because the entrance to the cave was close by. I waited. I couldn't read; I worried. From time to time, I called out, but Bobby didn't answer. When it started to become dark outside, I decided to drive back to the nearest town and ask for help. The local police said they couldn't look for Bobby that night but would form a party and begin the search the next morning."

Adam was becoming extremely uncomfortable. He silently wished he had the guts to tell John to stop, that he didn't want to hear any more.

"The local people were very considerate, offering me a

place to stay and encouraging me to remain hopeful, but as the days went by, I realized that, given the complexity of the cave, they probably wouldn't find him. After a week, the chief of the town told me that there was little chance Bobby had survived, and he was ending the search. Bobby was never found."

One day, when John and Bobby were throwing a ball after school, "Why do you hate Mr. Notkin so much?" Bobby asked John.

"He's gay," John told him.

"So? I'm gay too, and you don't hate me," Bobby said, catching the ball and tossing it back.

"You're different." John caught the tossed ball and put his arm around his friend. "I like you," and he brought Bobby closer. "I'll give you my baseball signed by Joe DiMaggio if you suck Notkin's dick," John told him in an offhand manner.

"You would?" Bobby said, disbelievingly, he had coveted that baseball ever since John had shown it to him.

"Notkin wants my ass," John said, and began whistling. "He more or less told me one day after gym class when he came into the locker room as I was undressing. You and I will meet him after class tomorrow and we'll 'do' him together." John bent his head and kissed his friend.

The following day, when Bobby walked into the classroom after classes had been dismissed for the day, he saw John talking with the teacher who was sitting on his desk, with John between the teacher's legs.

"He's all ready for you," John said as he unzipped the teacher's pants. Bobby went over and knelt down, reaching for the teacher's exposed crotch with his mouth. John leaned over his friend and, reaching in the back of the teacher's head, brought the teacher's face to his and kissed him.

"You fuckin' faggot," John hissed in the teacher's face. "I'm going to report you to the principal," and he turned to leave.

"Hold on there, John," the teacher said, leaving the desk and pulling up his pants.

"You're nothing but a fuckin' faggot," John repeated.

"I'll take you there myself," and the two of them left the classroom with Bobby wondering what was going to happen. He followed them to the principal's office and waited outside. A little while later, John opened the door, his face red, and marched past Bobby and down the hall. Bobby ran after him, catching up as John left the school building.

"What happened?" he asked, jogging to keep up with his friend.

"You're a fuckin' faggot, Bobby. If it weren't for you, I wouldn't have been expelled. The fuckin' principal believed that fuckin' teacher, that's what happened."

A few years later, while the two friends were lunching in the Four Seasons Restaurant, John suggested they explore some caves in Thailand.

"I want to go," John told his friend.

"It's risky, John," Bobby told him. "I don't."

"You're such a faggot. What can happen?" John called the waiter over.

"What kind of crap do you serve in this establishment?" he asked. "Take my steak back to the kitchen and bring me one that's edible." Turning to Bobby, "For the prices they charge, they ought to please their customers," he said. Over the years, Bobby had accustomed himself to John's abrupt — some would call it rude — manner. "I've bought the plane tickets, so you're coming with me," John informed his friend.

Arriving in Thailand, John and Bobby drove up to the entrance to the Tham Luang cave and parked. No other cars were there, which John had anticipated, as it was the off-season when guided tours had ended. They entered the cave, and John, who had inquired as to the location of the light switches, turned on the lights, illuminating the vast entrance and the crevices leading to the tunnels that he intended to explore. After they spent time walking around the chamber, John decided to take one of the tunnels and begin.

"Are you coming?" he asked.

"You go; I'll wait for you here," Bobby told him.

"My ass, you will; you're coming with me," and he put his arm around Bobby's shoulders and kissed him. "There will be more of that later. Come on," and he brought his friend with him as they entered one of the tunnels.

Using a map that he was given by one of the locals, John led them down a very narrow passage, passing openings to other tunnels and finally entered a chamber that was much smaller than the one at the entrance to the cave.

"You stay here," he told Bobby. "I need to go back …."

"What for? John, I don't want to be left here without you," Bobby said.

"Don't worry your sweet ass; I won't be but a few minutes," and he left. Twenty minutes later, John was at the entrance of the cave.

"Ever since I was expelled from school because of you, I've been resentful and full of rage," he ranted in the void. "I wanted revenge, and now I have it. Goodbye, Bobby." He walked over to the electrical panel and switched off the lights. Everything went dark. He stood in the entrance for over an hour, listening. At first, he heard muffled shouts, far off, but they became less and less distinct … until … nothing. Silence.

John then left and drove to the city. The next day, he took a flight back to Los Angeles.

"If it's okay with you, I'll turn in," Adam told John. "It's been a long day and I want to get back home; I'll be leaving tomorrow." Adam needed to get away, away from this place and away from John. John's telling him about how Bobby had died convinced him that Bobby's death and the deaths of others weren't accidents. He was beginning to suspect that John had something to do with how each had died. John hadn't appeared disappointed or distressed that they had died, leaving the two of them as the sole survivors.

"Stay for lunch and leave afterward. I'll make the chicken again, and for dessert, what about rhubarb pie? I grow it in my vegetable garden and it's ripe now."

Adam decided there would be no harm in John's suggestion and said goodnight. He entered his room and locked the door.

During the night, he had numerous dreams — really, nightmares — relating to his cabinmates. He would wake up thinking that he had been present when each had died. Throughout the night, he had a presentiment, why? He couldn't say, except that Irwin, Ed, Gregg, Billy, Tommy, and finally Bobby had all died under suspicious circumstances. Feeling as he did, caused him to sleep fitfully.

When he left his room in the morning, John was in the kitchen.

"Eggs?" John asked. "I'll fry a couple and you can eat them outside on the patio."

Adam didn't argue with him; he was still too worn down emotionally to object. Perhaps the cool morning air would revive him, he thought.

"If you need anything, I'll be in the kitchen preparing our lunch. I said I would roast a chicken and we'll have a fresh rhubarb pie for dessert. I hope you like spinach because that's what I'll make to go with the chicken."

"All sounds good to me," Adam told him. "I might take a walk."

After he left, Adam's mind reverted to thoughts of the boys in their cabin at camp. Was it purely coincidental that each had died in a bizarre way and that John always seemed to be present? John did tell him that he had remained friends with each of them, and that they had visited one another periodically over the years — until they died. But what was his reason for looking Adam up? They were never close, even as cabinmates.

These thoughts went through Adam's mind over and over as he walked along the cliffs. Two hours later, he returned to the cabin.

"Lunch is ready," John said as Adam entered. He sat down, but wasn't hungry. He couldn't wait for it to be over and leave.

"I've enjoyed your being here, Adam. Breast or leg? I'll give you a little of each. The spinach is quite good. I doctor it with an excellent sherry. Hope you like it," and he served Adam from one bowl, serving himself from another bowl. Perhaps Adam was being a little too suspicious, but he asked himself why John had served him from a different bowl than he had served himself. Why two bowls?

"Excuse me a moment; start without me." John got up and went to his bedroom.

To Adam, something was strange. The bowls looked the same … but were they?

"How's the chicken?" John asked when he returned. "And the spinach? I cooked up this recipe based on one I found in an early Martha Stewart cookbook."

Adam watched John, who appeared to be enjoying the meal.

"You never told me what you and your late wife did in France. Eat up, Adam; there's fresh rhubarb pie for dessert."

"We helped Jeanne's parents …."

"They lived there?"

"They were French, our reason for settling in their village."

"Where was that? Eat, don't let me distract you." Adam felt John was watching him.

"A village perché on the Côte d'Azur, just north of Nice. They owned a country inn in the village."

"Did it keep you busy?" John coughed and wiped his forehead with his napkin.

"As much as we wanted, I spent most of my time cycling in the region and sketching." John was looking decidedly uncomfortable. "Anything wrong?" Adam asked.

"I seem to be having a little trouble breathing; it'll pass."

It was not only John's breathing that was giving him trouble; Adam noticed that John lifted his fork with difficulty.

"John, are you okay?"

"I think I'll lie down, but you go on eating." John got up and began walking, but stumbled. Adam rushed over and helped him to the couch.

"It must have been something I ate; I'm finding it hard to … get my breath. Have you eaten your spinach?"

"John, you have to tell me what's been going on. Was there something in the bowl of spinach you served me?"

"I need … a … doctor."

"I won't call anyone until to tell me."

John couldn't move; to Adam, he appeared paralyzed.

"Spinach…," John said, and fell back, coughing, making harsh sounds when breathing.

"What are you saying?"

"I gave you … cough … cough … spinach … cough …," he whispered.

"John, whatever you served me, you ate. I suspected you have been lying to me. When you went to your bedroom, I switched bowls. You have to tell me what was in the bowl you meant me to eat, because you ate it." Adam looked at the man. John's mouth was open and drool was oozing from both sides of his mouth.

"Rhubarb," John whispered. "I … cooked … rhubarb leaves …." John's head rolled to one side; his breathing had become heavy and labored.

Adam googled rhubarb: After WW 1, some people in England died from ingesting the green leaf of rhubarb, believing it to be edible, not knowing it contained toxic levels of oxalic acid and anthrone glycosides.

Suddenly, Adam understood. John had eaten the green leaf of the rhubarb he had meant for Adam to eat. Unless Adam called for help, John would fall into an irreversible coma and eventually die, like the people had in England after World War 1. John had intended to kill him.

"Why did you want to kill me?" Adam asked, bewildered.

John turned and stared at Adam. "You … the others … cabin … behavior … sinful …." John raised himself to help his breathing, but slumped back. "Please … my doctor," he pleaded.

"Not until I know the whole story," Adam told him, watching John struggle.

"Same … behavior … myself … I … hated myself …."

"You killed the boys in our cabin," Adam told him.

"Killing them … would exorcize … me …." His breathing became more sporadic, his voice a mere rasping. "… free me …."

"And I was to be the last, was that your plan? You meant for me to eat the green leaf of the rhubarb?"

"You died … I … only … left; I … free." John was barely breathing, and his chest heaved.

"John, you're a bastard and don't deserve to live. You're nothing but a sloth. You thought eliminating others would release you? Killing our cabinmates, including me, you chose the easy way, instead of working on your problems." Adam paused to see if John was hearing what he was telling him.

John started coughing spasmodically. Adam handed

him a napkin. John coughed into it — blood. "I told you … everything; … a doctor," he gasped.

"No. You want release from what you tell me has been bothering you a lifetime? I'm going to set you free. I'm leaving. You're going to die — and gain your freedom."

Adam cleaned up the lunch dishes and put away all signs of his having been there. He heard John moan and scream from his prone position on the couch. Adam didn't have to restrain him because John couldn't move. The poison in the rhubarb greens was doing its job.

Adam packed his things and went over to the couch to see John one last time. He saw a pathetic creature, not a man worth saving.

He walked to the door and left.

ABOUT THE AUTHOR

E.P. Lande, born in Montreal, has lived in the south of France and now, with his partner, in Vermont, writing and caring for more than 100 animals.

Previously, as a Vice-Dean, he taught at l'Université d'Ottawa, and he has owned and managed country inns and freestanding restaurants.

Since submitting less than three years ago, more than 100 of his stories — many autofiction — and poems have found homes in publications on all continents except Antarctica. His story "Expecting" has been nominated for Best of the Net.

His debut novel, "Aaron's Odyssey", a gay-romantic-psychological thriller, has recently been published in London. Three of his other novels and a novella have also been accepted for publication.

5

LIFE AS A DECKHAND. AN ESSAY BY CHRISTOPHER JOHNSON

For three summers during college, I worked as a deckhand on steamships that carried iron ore from Duluth, Minnesota, to the voracious steel mills of Gary, Chicago, Cleveland, and other industrial cities on the southern shores of the Great Lakes. I did this because, being a union job, it paid very well and because my father was the traffic manager for the ships and could easily place me into a job. My father worked for U.S. Steel and was in constant contact with the ships, informing them what ports to go to and informing the ports when a particular ship would arrive. It was a complicated job, but he did it well. He did it well because he loved it. The job drew on his penchant for detail.

The previous summer, I had worked as a deckhand on the *Irving S. Olds*. Frankly, I don't remember much about it. I'd boarded the *Olds* only a few days after graduating from high school. I'd been all of seventeen years old. In the week leading up to boarding the *Olds*, I remember viewing the prospect of working on a ship with a mixture of dread and uncertainty. I had been very sheltered, growing up in a family that was, I felt, overly protective.

Yet I was also a contradiction. Deep inside me, I yearned for travel, for adventure, but I drew back from new experiences. Perhaps, in a sense, I feared rejection--that I would somehow not measure up to others' expectations. A kind of trepidation would kick in. I was a moth drawn to and fearful of the proverbial flame. In structured situations, I did well and was comfortable—such as in school, where the expectations were clear and approval for a job well done was always around the corner. But unstructured situations were a whole other thing. They stirred a sense of anxiety. What if I didn't measure up? What if? What if? And my mind would be off to the races, imagining the worst outcomes possible.

But, miracle of miracles, I had survived that summer

on the *Olds*. Everything had been a blur, but I had survived. I'd done as I'd been told. I'd carried out my duties quietly, obediently. I'd gained a smidgen of confidence. Now, as I prepared to board the *Arthur M. Anderson,* my anxiety had abated, my introversion had receded. I knew what to expect. I felt more ready to observe, to participate in the life of the *Anderson.*

A ship, as every seagoing author from Melville to Conrad has observed, is a self-contained and intricate mini-society—in this case, of 33 men. Thirty-three men with their cliques, likes, dislikes, and, in some cases, hatreds. Yet for all 33 souls, the main thing was the care and feeding of the ship. It took all kinds to run a ship. Suffice to say that both Richard Speck and Jack Kerouac had worked as deckhands.

As deckhands, our primary job was to batten down and remove hatches and to handle cables when the ship was pulling into the dock of one of the steel mills. But when we weren't pulling into or leaving a dock, our other primary responsibility was to care continually for the ship by chipping, sanding, and painting. It was hard work, but I liked it. I liked bending down and feeling the sun and the physical pleasure of driving the chipper into the old coat of paint and prepare the ship for the new coat. It was all about fending off the weather—efforts without which the ship would eventually become a rusty bucket.

I was one of four deckhands, and we were led by the boatswain—or bosun for short—who was primarily responsible for the docking and undocking and chipping and painting. On the *Anderson,* these men were all unique personalities. Larry was in his forties, with a round face and a round body and a Cheshire-cat smile. But his most salient characteristic was his deformed left hand and forearm. Larry had worked for years on the boats, and he had learned to compensate. Years of compensation had strengthened the muscles of his right hand and arm. When he shook my hand, he squeezed it until I winced. He handled the cables with aplomb, using his right hand to grab the cable and using his weakened left hand to guide the eye of the cable over the mooring.

We four deckhands shared one cabin—a tiny space in which we threw ourselves onto two bunk beds, each with a curtain to draw close to give ourselves some modicum of primacy. In those close quarters, we couldn't avoid knowing each other's business. Larry's business was dirty books. That was his "hobby," you might say. He opened his locker, and it was filled from floor to top with what you might call literature from the wrong side of town. He bought the books on the bumboat, which was a small vessel that came along the ships when they were docked and sold everything from Coke to cigarettes to the dirty books of which Larry was so enamored. I read a few. These were not *Lady Chatterley's Lover*—works of literature with flimsy clothing.

Then there was Buzz--Jim Buzhardt. He was my bunkmate. He had the upper bunk, and I inhabited the lower bunk. He'd done a tour of duty with the U.S. Marine Corps in Vietnam, which was gearing up toward the disaster it would soon become. This was 1967. Now he was working to save money to go to college. Buzz wore an ultra-neat crew cut and a tattoo on his muscular left bicep that displayed the insignia of the Marines. Like Lake Michigan during its calm interludes between storms, his quiet manner sat atop a steely intensity. Buzz introduced me to the poems of Robert W. Service, a British-Canadian poet who wrote about the Yukon and dreams lost and found among the gold mines of the North Country.

The fourth deckhand was Ernie Lundgren. Ernie had eyes like a falcon's and a mouth that turned down at the end into a perpetual look of displeasure. I came to think of Ernie as the Old Man of the Lakes. He'd worked on the lakes since the 1930s—since the Great Depression. He had always been a deckhand and never wanted anything more. He trained his eyes on those blocks of paint that were starting to fade and scab, and he attacked them with amazing ferocity. The important thing was to chip away the old paint on the deck of the *Anderson* so that we could give the ship a fresh new coat of paint to protect it from the unceasing elements. I sometimes wondered how much paint the *Anderson* absorbed in a year. It must have been hundreds of buckets—maybe even thousands! I wondered if Ernie were married. It was impossible to know. Ernie hardly ever talked.

Frank Bruno was the bosun—our boss. The most notable thing about Frank's physical appearance was his skin. It was ridged and soil-brown and beaten into submission by the sun and the rain and the snow. His belly was large and firm, his arms thick and beefy. On the second day after we left Gary on our way to Duluth, we were painting a portion of the deck with the distinctive red-brown color of the U.S. Steel fleet. Frank stared down at me as I applied the paint. "Nice work," he finally said, "but not much of it. You ain't Picasso or Rembrandt. Let's pick up the pace!" I got the message.

That night, in the deckhands' cabin, Larry, Buzz, Ernie, and I played poker. One of my suitcases served as the table on which we played. The game moved rapidly. If I was slow to state my bet, the three older men yelled at me to hurry the hell up! Larry and Buzz each had a small flask of whiskey that they sucked on, even though alcohol was strictly prohibited on board and was cause for immediate termination if it came to the attention of one of the officers. Larry and Ernie smoked, and soon the smoke had formed a thick, claustrophobic cloud. Buzz and I coughed and waved the smoke out of our faces. The three men played hurriedly, obsessively, even desperately.

The ante was a dollar. As the evening unrolled, Buzz won and Larry lost. After a couple of hours, Buzz was up a hundred dollars or more, and Larry was down the same amount. With each losing hand, Larry groaned. He cursed his cards. He looked at my small pile of winnings—about twenty bucks. He shook his head at how a dumb, stupid, naïve college kid could be outplaying him.

When it was Larry's deal, he used his good right hand and his malformed left hand to shuffle dexterously and deal rapidly. He smoked Camel after Camel. Unfiltered. He wiped the sweat that rolled down his forehead like drops of acid. "Crap!" he exclaimed after losing yet another hand. He slammed his cards down on the suitcase. He looked at the others, his eyes yellow.

By the third hour of the game, the atmosphere turned poisonous. Larry and Buzz were on the verge of being drunk. The cloud of cigarette smoke hung over the four of us like a stink bomb. After each loss, Larry threw down his cards. The beads of sweat on his forehead dripped into his eyes. Ernie said they should quit. Larry said, "No goddam way, not till I get my money back!"

After one more loss, Larry slammed his cards on the suitcase so hard that it made me jump. Larry looked at the neat pile of singles and fives and tens gathered like succulent sheep in front of Buzz. He stared at Buzz with evil eyes. Suddenly he shouted at Buzz, "Yer cheatin'! Yer dealin' from the bottom!"

"I'm not cheating, and you're drunk out of your mind!" Buzz said. I could see Buzz tighten his fists.

"Yera bastard!" Larry shouted. Suddenly he reached out and grasped the front of Buzz's shirt. "Give me my goddam money back!"

"Shove it up your ass!" Buzz squirmed out of Larry's grasp and pulled his fist back and glared at Larry. "You're so damn drunk you don't know what you're saying."

Larry got up and started to lunge at Buzz.

Ernie shot out his arm and pushed Larry back into his chair. He shoved his face up close to Larry's and said in a low voice, "He ain't cheating. The fact is--you're *drunk!* Get ahold of yourself, for God's sake!" Larry stared through the prism of alcohol at Ernie. I could see that he was afraid of Ernie. Larry turned away from Ernie and stared at the bunk next to where he was sitting. Ernie said, "Go out on deck and cool off for God's sake." He looked at Buzz and me. "This game is officially over."

Buzz shook his head and loosened up his fists. "What a jerk," he murmured.

Larry tottered out of the cabin and slammed the door. "He'll cool off," Ernie said. "I better go out there and make sure he don't fall overboard or some damn thing."

The next day, we deckhands were painting. We were *always* painting. Larry and Buzz refused to work together. After one day of their refusal to work together, Frank came into the deckhands' cabin and motioned to both of them to follow him. After about half an hour, they both returned. For the rest of the evening, they didn't look at each other. They didn't talk to each other. Larry slammed his curtain shut and read his dirty books. Buzz rambled out on deck and smoked and stared at the encroaching nightfall. The next day, Frank told Larry and Buzz to work together on painting the smokestack. Larry held the ladder while Buzz climbed up and painted. They didn't exchange a word. Not a word. But gradually they got the job done—painted the entire lower half of the smokestack until it gleamed under the sun. They did the job, all for the care and feeding of the *Anderson.*

One night, soon after the poker game, I saw Buzz alone out on deck. The sun was sinking in a blaze of glory toward the horizon in the west and lighting up the sky with bands of purple and red and orange that streamed across the sky. Buzz leaned against the cable that ran the length of the ship. I walked up to him. Buzz nodded at the sinking sun and the blazing sky and said, "She's a beauty, isn't she?"

We leaned together on the cable, each with one leg up on the bottom cable. Buzz turned to me and surreptitiously slipped a flask out of his front pocket and offered it to me. "Here," he said. "Have a snort." As furtively as possible, I put the flask to my lips and drank. The whiskey burned its way down my throat and threw flames into my belly. I coughed. I looked at Buzz and said, "Larry sure was a jerk that night—the poker night."

Buzz snaked a snort of his own out of the flask and looked at the blazing orange and red ribbons that dragooned across the sky. "Oh," he said, "these things happen. He just had too much to drink. He's not a bad guy. Frank did the right thing to make us work together after that happened. You can't let things like that fester. It's not good for the sake of the ship if you let things fester like that. That's what makes Frank a good boss. He knows what he's doing."

I looked at Buzz. I envied his self-assurance, his air that he knew exactly what was what. He looked at me and said, "Kid, you're coming along, you know. You probably don't even know it, but you've learned a lot of stuff out here that'll do you good." I knew it was true. I'd been on the *Anderson* for a month now, and I'd started to absorb the ways of the ship. It was more than painting or handling cables. It was learning secrets about the way things worked, the ways people worked. I'd learned to take soundings, or measuring the amount of water in the tanks of the ship. Frank had let me handle the winches, which controlled the cables, while he watched. I'd learned to handle the thick hoses efficiently when we were cleaning the hold after the Hulett shovels at Gary had scooped up the iron ore and transported it to the steel mills. "I hated it the first few weeks," I said, "but now I kind of like it. I like Frank and Ernie. I've even gotten used to Larry."

"Him and his dirty books," Buzz said with a chuckle. He shook his head. "You know, a guy like that--with that hand of his, you know--he's done all right. He's had to deal with a lot of stuff in his life. That night of the poker, I was ready to knock him on his ass. That was wrong. I lost my cool, mostly because I had a little too much out of this here flask. I lost my cool, and I shouldn't have done that. I was mad at myself after that. That is the big thing they drive into you when you first get in the Marines—don't lose your cool."

Buzz paused. "I don't exactly feel sorry for the man. Another thing I learned in the Marines is that it doesn't do any good to feel sorry for other people. But I know it's been pretty tough for him over the years. You'll notice that he doesn't have too many buddies out here on this boat." He paused. "That's what I've noticed out here," he continued. "A lot of these sailors—they don't really have friends, even though they work and live together all the time."

"I noticed that, too" I said. I paused and then asked, "Are you going to stay on the boats?"

"Hell no. I'm saving every nickel I can out here. I've got the G.I. Bill, so the government will pay for me to go to school. I'm going to go to the University of Minnesota, and I'm going to major in business. And then I'm going to start a business of some kind. I don't know what it'll be, but I know that's what I'll do. I was only 18 when I signed up for the Marines, and the only thing I wanted was to get away from home and make something of myself. I didn't have a plan when I went into the Marines. But gradually I learned. I learned that I'm not especially in love with taking orders. I want to run things. You know, I could start a painting business or something related to computers—they're going to be big. But whatever it is, I'm gonna learn everything I can about running a business. I'm gonna be like a sponge."

I stared at Buzz. I'd never heard anyone be so definite. Buzz's dream was like a tree in a forest that you could wrap your arms around. The dream surrounded Buzz and somehow made him more real. I stared at Buzz and felt myself so unformed, so directionless.

"So what do you think about that, eh?" Buzz grinned. "I'm a man with a plan. And if that doesn't turn out--well, I'll think of something else to do!" We laughed together and took swigs from Buzz's handy flask and threw our laughs overboard into the surrounding waters.

That evening, after supper, I walked onto the deck of the *Anderson*. To the east, I could see, miles away, a stretch of sand, yellow-white against the stark blue sky. This, I would later learn, was Sleeping Bear Dunes in Michigan. The dunes were 300 feet high, but from this distance of many miles, it was a tiny strip. The *Anderson* moved inexorably north, and the dune slowly slipped into the distance. It had been there, and now it was disappearing. The crew was being propelled forward, and in the meantime, the earth was spinning on its axis.

The next morning, Frank took me aside and said he wanted to talk to me before we started work that day. I stared at Frank, who wore the years in deep crevasses that crawled across his face. Frank's nose bent down like a broken golf club, and his skin had absorbed the rays of the sun and transmogrified them into thick, tough leather. Behind Frank's rough and weathered exterior, though, his eyes were steady. He looked at me and said, "Young feller, do you have a radio?"

"Aye, sir."

"Does it get a strong signal?"

I nodded.

"Well, every morning, I want you to turn on that radio

and get the sporting news and the regular news, and I want you to pour a cup of fresh coffee and bring it to me and give me as good a rundown on the day's news as you can." This would mean carrying Frank's coffee the length of the ship because Frank's cabin was toward the bow of the *Anderson.* "Do you think you can handle that, young feller?"

I nodded. The next morning, I did as Frank had asked. I listened to the radio for a bit, ate breakfast, poured a cup of coffee for Frank, and transported it to him.

When I opened the door to Frank's cabin, it was like entering a home away from home. Frank had curtains over the porthole that looked out onto Lake Michigan. He had a matching bedspread. On his dresser stood neatly arranged photographs of a woman and a young man and young woman—Frank's wife and children, I assumed. Frank was sitting in an easy chair in the corner of the cabin when I entered. I handed Frank the cup of coffee, and he said, "Thank you, young feller. Set yourself down." I sat on a metal chair in front of Frank's small desk. "So do you like it out here on the lake?" Frank asked.

"I hated it at first. It was so confusing--so overwhelming."

"That's good. That's the way it's supposed to be." Frank paused. "I saw you looking at those pictures. Those are my wife, Margaret, and my two children, Frank Jr., and Annette." He looked at me. "Now tell me about the baseball yesterday." I knew that Frank was from Minnesota, so I reported that the Twins had beaten the White Sox.

Frank said, "Well, that's all fine and good. The Twins are loaded. They have Harmon Killebrew and Bob Allison —all these strong guys who can hit the ball a mile. But can they turn a double play? Winning—it's all in the details. You know what I like about baseball, young feller? It's pointless. That's the *beauty* of it. You have all these wonderful athletes, and you have the beautiful shape of the baseball diamond. It has a magical geometry. And there's no *point* to it all! If you win, you don't inherit a million dollars. If you lose, the world don't come to an end. There's no point to it! That's what makes it *beautiful.*"

Frank paused for a moment and looked closely at me. "You know," he said, "I seen something in you. You're gonna be a good worker, but your mind wanders. You need to learn to—and I mean this in a way meant to be helpful—you need to learn to keep your head in the game, like a ballplayer needs to learn to do." I nodded. I knew what he meant. He said. "Keep yer eyes open. Yer workin' on the most precious bodies of water on the earth—the Great Lakes. After yer watch, take a moment to step out on deck and admire their beauty." He mused for a moment. "And another thing. Yer gonna be criticized out here. *I'm* gonna criticize you. But don't take it to heart. We're just tryin' to make you better at yer job. It's all about makin' the ship work better and takin' care of the ship so she is seaworthy for a long time far into the future."

Frank stared at me. "Cuz you see, it's us against the elements out here. The elements are all tryin' and strainin' to destroy this here ship. During a storm—and yer sure to encounter one out here sooner or later—well, I believe in God, but during one of the fearsome storms that come up, especially on Lake Superior, God ain't gonna protect us, that's for sure. We gotta do it ourselves. Yer on yer own out here during a storm. So like I said, you gotta keep yer head in the game." He paused. "Now, do you have any questions for me?"

"Yes, sir," I said. "How long have you been sailing out here on the lakes?"

"Well, I started when I was 19 years old. I was just out of high school. But then there was World War II, and I served in the U.S. Navy for the duration. I got out of the service in 1946, and I decided to go back on the lake steamers, and I been here ever since. Twenty-two, twenty-three years, I guess, if you add it all up." He paused. "Well, listen, he said. "I'm all talked out for one day. So let's get out there and paint this goddam tub!"

More weeks passed, and then it was my last trip, at the end of which I would leave the *Anderson* and return to school. We had left Duluth behind and were well into Lake Superior when Frank called us deckhands together and said, "Bad weather report. It's gonna blow." To the northeast, the clouds were accumulating and obliterating the sun, and the waves were beginning to rise up in anger. Frank had told me earlier in the summer that we would experience a good blow at least once before I left the *Anderson*, and this was going to be it.

Normally, when we deckhands tightened the battens that held the hatches in place, we tightened only every other one. But now the four of us went back on deck and secured every batten to take sure that the hatches didn't slide out of place. That was the greatest danger to the ship--that the terrible forces of the storm would move the hatches and allow water into the hold.

We finished securing the hatches. Frank told us to clear any coiled ropes, stray chippers, or paint brushes off the deck. The waves began to leap at the ship, and I could feel the vessel start to rock back and forth. Frank told me to go to the deckhands' cabin and make sure nothing was left loose. I grabbed my radio and some other paraphernalia off the dresser and shoved it into one of the drawers. I removed toothpaste and toothbrushes and other toiletries from the head and shoved them into the drawers of the dresser. I closed and tightened the porthole, for water would swamp the cabin otherwise.

I climbed into my bunk. I could hear the anger of the lake, feel the *Anderson* rocking back and forth, back and forth. I lay in my bunk, waiting, while the other three more experienced deckhands helped Frank secure anything else on the ship that needed securing. I heard the roar of the waves and the attack of lightning and thunder and the scream of the wind as it pelted the *Anderson*. The *Anderson* was rolling—five degrees, then ten degrees--tipping inexorably from side to side. I felt bile began to build in my stomach. The other deckhands came in and stripped off their rain gear and retreated to their bunks. Buzz said, "It's gonna be hell out there!"

The bile gathered in my belly. I closed my eyes and felt the rolling of the ship and my bunk rising and falling like a chaotic baby's carriage. I felt the acidic bile churning in my lower intestine. "Oh, my God," I whimpered. I clutched my pillow as I felt the ship roll back and forth. I felt the bile moving toward my esophagus. "Oh my God, oh my God," I moaned. The wind attacked the vessel, and the waves rolled the *Anderson* back and forth, back and forth, and the bile worked its way up through my esophagus. I clamped his eyes shut and grasped the metal undergirding of his bunk bed. I felt the bile enter my throat as the ship careened back and forth.

Suddenly I catapulted myself out of the bunk and half-raced and half-crawled to the head as I felt myself thrown back and forth by the force of the rolling ship. I slammed open the toilet and let loose, coughing, sputtering. I wiped my mouth, tasted the horrendous acidic taste, stood up just enough to be able to look into the mirror. I was ghostly pale—alabaster white—so white that I looked like a corpse. I wanted to be dead! Frank had been right---there was no God during a storm on Lake Superior.

I half-ran, half-fell back to my bunk. At the same time, Buzz leaped out of his bunk and opened up the porthole just enough to see out. Over Buzz's shoulder, I could see the angry, roiling waves of Lake Superior. The porthole descended as the *Anderson* rolled deeper toward the waters. The waves were angry, attacking. I knew that the waves were crashing and washing over the bow of the ship. I got up. Ernie screamed at me, "Get back into yer bunk right away!" Ernie yelled at Buzz, "Close that goddam porthole, for Christ's sake!" Buzz slammed it shut.

Back in my bunk, I was exhausted. I picked the bits from around my mouth and wiped them away with the bandanna in my rear pocket. The ship continued to roll. Tears sprouted in my eyes. Would this never end!? I heard the angry gods pummel the *Anderson*, slamming it, rocking it back and forth, attacking the steel hull. The gods were angry that the *Anderson* had ventured into their territory. They were relentless and without mercy. Poseidon roiled the waves with his mighty hands and tossed the waves over the ship. Would the ship crack in two? I sank into fear and felt the pile build up once more in my belly. It was the worse moment of my entire life, and it was never-ending. I staggered to the head again, released again, looked again at my face in the mirror. It was dead-white. Tears crept down my cheeks. I stumbled back to my bunk, clutched my pillow, fought against the bile. There was nothing left in my belly.

Gradually, I felt the *Anderson* roll a little less, the force of the waves begin to abate, the howl of the wind grow a little less fierce. I clutched my pillow. Disregarding what Ernie had said, Buzz leaped out of his bunk and opened the porthole a crack and looked out onto the angry lake. It was marginally less angry. The rolling was less steep, less sickening. A touch of light punctuated the clouds. The ship kept rolling, but less severely. I clutched my pillow, fought the bile building up in my belly once again. I turned away so that the others would not see me huddling in my bunk. I didn't want them to see me. I sniffled and clutched my pillow. The ship rolled, but not so severely. The wind roared outside, but less angrily. Poseidon had settled down. He wasn't so angry any more. The others arose from their bunks.

Buzz grabbed me. "The worst is over," he said. "Put your rain gear on. Let's see what the damage is." We walked down the interior hallway of the aft cabin to the hatch that led out onto the deck. The ship still rolled, but now that I was on my feet, the rolling didn't seem to affect me so much. Lake Superior was settling down, the rolling less pronounced. We looked out, and we could see the bow of the *Anderson* cut its way through the thick, gray waves. The *Anderson* battled its way forward, and it was winning. The hatches protecting the hold had not budged. The battens had stayed secure. The work we had done was good. Water had not seeped into the hold. Buzz put his hand on my shoulder and said, "Fun, eh?"

Larry patted me on the shoulder and said, "Look at it this way, kid. You lost five ugly pounds." I managed a pathetic chuckle.

As the lake settled down, I retreated to the deckhands' cabin, threw myself onto my bunk. Almost immediately, I fell asleep. I slept through the night as the *Anderson* made it way to the Soo Locks at Sault Ste. Marie—the locks that led from Lake Superior to Lake Huron.

The next morning, Buzz grabbed my big toe and shook it until I woke up. "Time to go to work!" he said. "We'll be going through the Soo locks soon!" We walked out onto the deck, and Frank propelled Buzz and me onto the dock on the bosun's chair. We threw the eye of each cable over a mooring and watched as the ship was slowly lowered to bring it to the level of St. Marys River, which would lead into Lake Huron.

Overlooking the locks was an observation deck, filled with spectators. I regarded them. I remembered when I had made my first trip through the locks, and I had desperately wished that I'd been among the spectators watching the men on the *Anderson* do their work. In three months, things had changed. I was part of the crew of the *Anderson*. I felt apart from those spectators. The world of the *Anderson* had absorbed me in those three months. I was an integral part of the ship. I knew that in two more days, I would be leaving the ship, and I felt bittersweet. The things that had happened, the men I had lived with and worked with for three months—they had become part of who I was. I felt myself different in some way that I could not articulate but that felt as real and solid as the deck of the *Anderson*. This thing—sailing—had gotten into my bones in some mysterious way. The ways of the ship had infiltrated my psyche. I felt different from the spectators now-- part of a separate world that had slowly accepted me and changed me. I'd become part of something larger than myself—a mission to care for the *Anderson* and preserve and protect it.

Two days later, the *Anderson* drew near Gary, where the giant Hulett shovels would dig the iron ore out of the bowels of the ship and dump it into railroad cars that would transport the ore to the insatiable steel mills. I ate my breakfast and, for the last time, transported a cup of coffee to Frank. He was waiting for me. He said, "So, it's your last day on the *Anderson*. You're abandoning us to our fates, eh?" He grinned at me. I happened to look at the three photographs on Frank's dresser. "Do you remember their names?" Frank asked.

"Yes, sir," I answered. "Margaret, your wife; your daughter, Annette; and your soon, Frank Jr. What do your children do now, Frank?"

"Oh, they have their own lives, as children have a habit of doing. Annette is married and has two children, and she teaches third grade in a small town in western Minnesota. Frank, Jr., works for an engineering firm in Minneapolis." Frank lifted himself from his easy chair and walked over to the dresser and picked up each photograph and looked at it. The crevasses that crisscrossed his face looked deeper than ever, and his eyes were hooded by the accumulated years. He looked at me and shook his head ever so slightly. He said, "I missed things when they were growing up. I made it to their graduations and weddings and all the important stuff. But being out here, I missed the day-to-day stuff—wiping their noses, playing ball, that kind of thing. Margaret basically raised them." I looked at him—at the deep lines in his leathery skin and the aging eyes. "In many ways, it's a good life," Frank murmured. He paused. "But it can be a lonely life."

For the last time, I rode the *Anderson* into Gary. Each of the men I had worked with that summer—Frank and Buzz and Larry and Ernie—shook my hand and wished me the best. Even Larry said, "You done a good job this summer, kid." I felt more strongly than I had ever felt that something bound me to each of these four men.

I descended the ladder and stood on the dock and looked up at the enormous Hulett shovels unloading ore from the *Anderson*. The operator, sitting in a cab above the shovel, catapulted the shovel forward on a track until the shovel stood directly over one of the open hatches. He released the shovel, sent it plunging into the hold, and I heard the shovel close, grasping hundreds of pounds of iron ore.

The operator raised the shovel and drove backwards and released the ore into a waiting freight car. I turned, and a cab was waiting to carry me into Gary and the South Shore Railroad station, where I would catch a train for Chicago.

As I rode in the cab through the fantastic chaos of the steel mill, the memories of the summer burrowed into me--memories so powerful that they infiltrated my bones and my muscles and pounded through my veins.

. . .

ABOUT THE AUTHOR

I'm a writer based in the Chicago area. I've done a lot of different stuff in my life. I've been a merchant seaman, a high school English teacher, a corporate communications writer, a textbook editor, an educational consultant, and a free-lance writer.

I've published short stories, articles, and essays in The Progressive, Snowy Egret, Earth Island Journal, Chicago Wilderness, American Forests, and other journals and magazines.

In 2006, the University of New Hampshire Press published my first book, This Grand and Magnificent Place: The Wilderness Heritage of the White Mountains.

My second book, which I co-authored with a prominent New Hampshire forester named David Govatski, was Forests for the People: The Story of America's Eastern National Forests, published by Island Press in 2013.

6

THE PUGILIST, A STORY
BY RICHARD KORST

My wife is a warrior, a fighter, the consummate pugilist.

While her fight occurs outside the ropes, she bears the boxer's scars earned and amassed in the ring, some visible, others undetected. She's received radiation, endured several rounds of chemo, been poked, prodded, and bled yet, each day, each moment in the ring, she obstinately confronts her menacing and relentless adversary.

She has been knocked to the canvas countless times, arising after each potential knockout blow, the referee's count perilously approaching ten as she defiantly points her gloves skyward, screaming, "I'm good. I'm good. I can keep fighting!"

Her daughters painfully watch her staggering drop in weight class from light-heavyweight to lightweight and internalize their fears; afraid of her startling transformation and, quietly, fearful of their own fate, their possible future battles. Despite their concerns, they proceed like the trainer's cornermen, tending to the stumbling fighter's wounds, offering water and encouragement, grasping tightly to the white towel; unwilling, like their mother, to give up the fight.

My duties happen behind the scenes, preparing her for the fight, ensuring she has the energy, the doctor's care to sustain her battle. Silently, each night, I pray to God, not for His miraculous intervention but for relief, a respite from my wife's daily struggles. To date, my prayer has not crossed His desk, nor do I expect a quick reply, but each day provides another opportunity for hope. I'm not angry with God, hate Him, or even blame Him. If I did, how could I explain all the world's suffering and pain? How could I selfishly think my prayers would carry more weight than the millions of others offered and deferred?

No, my God sits next to me, outside the ring in the first row, His head bowed, His eyes closed. His arm drapes around my shoulders, and He weeps with me, touched by my wife's indomitable spirit, yet pained by His inability to ease her pain in this earthly realm.

The bell tolls once more, she rises from her corner stool, battered, bruised, but unflinching, circles her combatant, spits adamantly, and waves them in for another round. My wife is a warrior, a fighter, a pugilist, a cancer casualty, and a cancer survivor.//

ABOUT THE AUTHOR

Rick is a husband, father of twins, brother to two sisters and a brother, and son of parents who emigrated to the United States from Austria after World War II.

A graduate of the University of Illinois (Urbana-Champaign) with an MBA from the University of Texas in Austin, Rick spent over forty years in the corporate world, specializing in Human Resources.

Rick writes when a story hits him and his work can be found in Spillwords, The Last Line, and Horrortree along with a book titled "Clarence Earns His Wings Again"

His wife Kate, two dogs, Bailey and Sawyer, and sometimes their daughters (when not in school), Katie and Chloe make their home in Illinois.

7

THE WRECK OF SKEETER'S
BEER CAVE. A STORY
BY MICHAEL GIGANDET

I heard the car coming before I ever saw it, that peculiar whine and whir rubber tread makes when accelerating on asphalt blistering under an unrelenting August sun in Tennessee. It's a sound you can't mistake for anything else, even if it's punctuated by the banging of a rusted-out tailpipe. The car straightened the curve onto our street and laid a streak of rubber on the pavement before it jumped the curve and landed on my mother's rose bush, crunching the plastic trellis she got on sale at Walmart. The driver shoved the stick into reverse, backed onto the road and cut the engine. The car, a '58 or '59 Cadillac, considering the surfboard-sized fins rising off the rear fenders and all the chrome devoted to the behemoth's decoration, ran on for a few seconds, making popcorn sounds as it settled into place like a hen waddling up a nest in the dust on a summer afternoon.

The car's antenna whipped the air like an out-of-control fishing rod while the driver reached up and stopped the large dice cubes dangling from the mirror in mid-swing like he was pinching something floating by in the air.

He was wearing aviator sunglasses with mirrors for lenses. When he got out of the car, he whipped his sunglasses off as if he realized he needed to examine something with unprotected eyes.

"Did you miss me?" he shouted across the yard to where I sat in my boxers, in a lawn chair under a Sugar Maple, drinking coffee out of a mug in the shape of a Beagle's head, and waiting for my mother's Chihuahua, Elvis, to move his bowels so I could go back inside and do nothing in there.

"I thought about you every day." Raymond Poteete may have been the only person in Needmore I didn't think about at least once during my vacation in the wasteland they call Afghanistan. "My mother's gonna kick your ass."

Raymond walked around to the front of the Caddy, snatched a piece of the trellis from the jaws of the bumper and dropped it next to the bush.

"She won't if I get her a new one before she gets home."

"You drunk?"

"Too early in the day. I got my ethical standards."

I wondered where a guy like Raymond Poteete ever heard the word "ethical." Not in this town, which is what I would call a two-syllable culture as in *redneck* or *rustic*, depending upon my attitude. Three-syllable people leave Needmore as soon as they can, telling people that they're from Had Enough. We never did have a movie theatre. I knew the town was going downhill when a take-out pizza parlor, a wheelchair rental shop, and a thrift store opened on the public square while I was in high school. It was worse now. I couldn't count all of the vacant storefronts on the square when my mother drove me home from the airport.

"Just tell her that flower bed was destroyed by a Cadillac once owned by The King."

My mother's passion for Elvis was well known in this community, along with everybody else's passions, doings and misdoings.

Our house was an unofficial Elvis museum since you couldn't look in any direction or at any piece of furniture with a flat space on it without seeing something related to Elvis, a photograph, Elvis and Priscilla salt and pepper shakers, an Elvis bobble head which started singing "Love Me Tender" anytime you walked by its electronic eye.

"I'm surprised Elvis ever let that car go."

Detroit could've made another car out of the steel in the Caddy's bumpers which capped each end of the car like monolithic bookends. There were no hubcaps on the wheels, and although it was summer, at least two of the tires were snow tires.

"I heard you's home." Raymond was wearing a Hawaiian shirt, shorts and sandals with white socks.

The Corps gave me two weeks' leave and a lance corporal patch in return for not embarrassing them over there, so I came home to visit. Except for my mother, no one I ran into seemed to have missed me which was not surprising since my friends had fled as soon as graduation commencement was over. I was already at the stage of homecoming where you begin thinking you'd rather be back with the guys and the unit, talking about how wonderful home is and how you wish you were there.

Raymond snatched up a lawn chair and tried to open it with one electric snap of his wrist, but the hinges were rusted tight, and he began to wrestle with it first with both hands and then with a knee. I ignored him out of politeness.

"Doing anything?" he asked.

I did have a plan for the day. I slept late that morning which I considered healthful, and that night I planned to drink the rest of my mother's beer on her back porch in the dark while contemplating the meaning of life and listening to the cicadas buzzing like sons of bitches in the trees and the neighborhood dogs taking turns barking at each other, debating who could beat up who or discussing their plans for an animal revolt. A man who does not plan ahead risks spending Time like it was easy money and not having anything to show for it.

"You got any plans?" I asked, although I did not expect him to have any, considering that Raymond had always been the kind of guy who does what other people in Needmore are doing, like drinking beer down at the river, drinking beer while fishing in said river, drinking beer while sitting around trying to think of something to do.

"Naw," he said and joined me in watching Elvis search the yard for an inspiring patch of ground to conduct his business.

"Would you rather be killed by a pack of wolves or a pack of dogs?" Raymond asked which was the kind of question you'd expect from a guy who'd failed first and third grades.

I can honestly say that in my entire 19 years of living and out of all the things I ever thought to think about, I have never contemplated this question, so I said. "I never thought about it."

"Pick wolves. Wolves kill for food, but dogs kill for fun. Your wolf is just doing what God told him to do, so it's a kind of religious way to die."

Sometimes Raymond was capable of profound thought, even if he didn't know it.

Again, I wondered whether I should have gone to college like my friends and spun my wheels there while I tried to get some traction in my life and figure things out as I set out on the road to responsible citizenship. But wasn't that why I joined the Marine Corps in the first place? I was just passing the time in a different way than my friends.

I sure as hell didn't plan on spending my leave with Raymond who I had to admit always was a cheerful person even if he had been the hanger-on kid throughout our adolescence.

"You should congratulate me," he said. Since I couldn't think of anything that Raymond could do that would call for congratulations, I didn't say anything; I just looked at him.

"I finished summer school today."

"You still in school?" I asked. The man was 19 years old.

"I graduated high school last May with a diploma and everything, but they said they'd take it back if I didn't go to summer school for reading and such."

"Well congratulations." I suspected they gave him a diploma to get rid of him.

"We could celebrate, but nobody's around," he said, sounding down about it, which seemed sad to me because he was stuck here in Needmore forever, and I was just visiting. Things were going to happen to me; soon, I was going to be somewhere else.

"Yeah, I hadn't planned on everybody being gone," I said, not even considering Raymond, who was sitting right there next to me.

The truth is, even if some friends were still here, nobody did the things we used to do. You just don't go away for a year and then come back and expect everything to be the same. The world goes on without you, but nobody teaches you that which is probably one of those lessons you grow into learning as your life happens to you. Maybe that's why I preferred my mother's couch to sleeping in my bedroom with the baseball posters and model airplanes; it didn't feel right anymore, and I'd slept in a lot worse places.

When Raymond didn't say anything, I asked, "What happened to the friendly girls?" Raymond would know about the town's romantic goings-on since he was still in communication with the remains of our social circle via his educational pursuits.

"Ah…this and that," he said. "Not much cooking there."

"What about that Jackson girl?

"Somebody gave her the clap and she got the cure and religion at the same time. Last time I went to see her she wanted to wash my feet and pray."

"Sam's sister?"

"Pregnant," he said, and then in a fit of remembrance. "You remember Sherry Hunsucker?!"

Absolutely, I said with more enthusiasm than I felt good about.

"She's a stripper down in a fancy club in Atlanta."

I felt the air let out of me like a leaking balloon. "Not much happening I guess."

"Was there ever anything happening here?" he asked, which was pretty insightful of him. Nothing much ever did happen in Needmore if you weren't drinking cheap beer with your friends down at the river or sitting in a car sliding one hand up the thigh and one hand into the blouse of one of the friendly girls. I'd been thinking that was what I wanted, but it wasn't that at all; I was empty.

Everything I believed about myself and everything I felt for the people I knew just seeped out of me when I wasn't paying attention. You go away and at first you think about those things a lot, and all the while they're getting away from you, being replaced with other things to think about like the moment you realize a bullet not meant for you sounds like an angry bee on a mission and the dull thud you hear way up ahead of you will always be followed by the sound of people running and other things you'll never forget.

"I got this idea," Raymond said. He'd heard of a place on the far side of the next county where they partied hard and didn't stand on ceremony when it came to drinking age restrictions.

"They say the guy what runs it is really selling shine out of his car trunk. This place is just a front."

And that's how everything that happened at Skeeter's got started.

WE DROPPED off the highway into what passed for a parking lot at Skeeter's Beer Cave, which turned out to be an old gas station out on Highway 41 near the county line, one of those abandoned stations from the 1950s before the interstates came and bypassed everything (which may also explain why Needmore became the Had Enough we love today).

It was that time of night when the lightning bugs begin to rise up out of the grass and float around, twinkling hello to each other like they were happy they survived another day and were ready to hook up and celebrate. They reminded me of childhood when I thought they were magical, and I hoped we weren't running over any of them since the parking lot was more grass than gravel.

"We'll definitely get beer here," Raymond said, nodding at the pick-up trucks in the parking lot. "It's a good sign."

Over the door, a yellow light bulb dangled from a cord, illuminating a sign which read "No Rif Raf", the extra "f" apparently being discretionary. A dead cat, desiccated and flat as a doormat, lay in the gravel. Festive music and the sounds of camaraderie flowed out the windows, which were propped open with a beer bottle, a phone book and a broken umbrella.

The festive noises competed with the sound of cicadas in the trees, buzzing and pulsating, rising and falling not unlike waves sweeping upon a beach. My mother told me that if you put your hand on the bark of a tree the cicadas in that tree will all go silent at once, but I never could get them to do that for me.

I walked in, scanning the place, taking it all in without making eye contact. I was not surprised to see an assortment of drunks, wife beaters and animal rapers scattered around in various stages of moral and physical deterioration. This was the kind of place where patrons wear their ball caps inside, smoke unfiltered cigarettes, spit snuff juice into plastic soda bottles and belch and fart without feeling the need to say "excuse me". I felt them watching us like in a western movie when a cowboy enters a saloon and the piano stops while everybody sizes him up before the piano starts up again.

WE MOUNTED stools at the bar, which was actually three scrap doors lying end to end on fifty-gallon oil drums.

Mr. Skeeter was apparently tight with his money, considering how little he wasted on décor, which I would describe as "post-nuclear-holocaust garden party" because of the mixture of mismatched card tables and lawn chairs that filled his establishment. There was one big metal table, which somebody must have stolen from the Holiday Inn swimming pool out at the interstate, with a hole in the middle where a giant umbrella could be inserted. A stage of sorts occupied one end of the room for karaoke night, which was on Tuesdays according to the sign next to the stage: "Karryoak Nite Ever Tuesday". Beside the stage was a recliner with the stuffing coming out of the arms and headrest, and in that chair sat the only female in attendance, a woman with blond hair piled higher than Dolly Parton's with breasts the size of her head imprisoned in a glittery blouse stretched so tight that the buttons stood up on edge. She wore cowboy boots, and it looked like she had recently skinned her knee, most likely from falling down drunk somewhere.

"What do you peckerheads want?" the bartender asked like he knew we were underage and was fixing to kick us out of the place, which, considering the place was a dump, would be especially insulting when you think about it.

"A couple of beers," Raymond said, adding, "We're parched…Been working on tobacco all day."

Anyone with a lick of sense could see that neither of us had an ounce of sunburn on our faces and hands from cutting tobacco under a cruel August sun. But if you had any sense, you wouldn't be in a place like that, so I chalked up Raymond's biographical license to the colorful narrative he thought necessary for us to have credibility among that crowd. Raymond smiled to show the bartender how nice we were, but the guy looked at him like he was a bug who'd just asked him the time of day. "Yes sir, just some cold ones," Raymond said. "…after a hard day's labor in which we earned lots of cash we want to spend with you."

The bartender, who looked like Popeye the Sailor, and may have been a sailor considering the anchor and mermaid tattoos on his forearms, walked away, but he didn't say "get the hell out" which I considered a positive sign. Still, it was against the law of the land for a 19-year-old to buy a beer in America, even though the taxpayers had just spent a few thousand dollars training this underage drinker how to efficiently kill bad guys with a machine gun whenever they got a hard-on for somebody.

The bartender pulled two bottles of beer from a styrofoam ice chest with a cartoon on the side of a leaping bass wearing a straw hat and sunglasses and slammed them down on the bar so hard that 50 cents' worth of beer frothed down the neck like volcanic lava.

We reached for our beers, but he pulled them back. "Got any money peckerheads?"

Of course, I thought, you think we just came in here without money? I had enough sense not to say that.

Raymond did, or something close to it, and I immediately felt the tension ratchet up on the cosmic intensity meter. I'll say this for the Corps: I'd learned to sense when things weren't right or when I needed to get ready. Maybe I wouldn't know what to get ready for, but I knew to tense up and prepare for whatever was coming at me. God knows life can happen to you fast in moments like these.

"Show me." The bartender grinned at Raymond like he'd just caught him lying.

Raymond opened his wallet and thumbed the bills inside. "All 20s," he said. "Hope you can make change here." I watched the bartender's hands without letting on about it.

The bartender looked at him like he was thinking of something malevolent to say but couldn't find the right insult when Raymond smartened up and said, "And we tip generously for good service." The cosmic stress meter went to zero when the bartender grinned like he was in pain, said "Okay big spender" and pushed the bottles over like we'd been buddies all along.

Although we had a kind of truce with the bartender, we gulped the beer down in case he changed his mind about serving us. The bartender stuffed Raymond's $20 bill into his jeans and made change out of a cigar box.

There was a television over the bar, but it was a black and white model and the picture rolled up over the screen every 45 seconds. No one cared, preferring to frequent a juke box which specialized in truck driving songs from the 1950s. From the look of the clientele, you weren't going to find any Sonic Youth, Led Zeppelin or Liz Phair on there. While I was away, I'd heard music I had never heard before, lots of it I guess, because it occurred to me that my musical tastes had changed.

Thanks to Raymond, our truce didn't last long. If you're a stranger in an establishment like Skeeter's, the one thing you don't want to do is to call extra attention to yourself. It isolates you, and predators look for that. Raymond didn't know about that rule and asked, "Pardon me, barkeep, could we have a menu?"

"Hey, these peckerheads want to eat supper!" The bartender bellowed to the drunks at the card tables who began making the sounds you might hear in a crowded barnyard at dinner time while a herd of donkeys engaged in an orgy, all of which seemed appropriate to me considering that crowd.

"Well how about a frosty glass?"

"We ain't got no glasses," the bartender said. "They got broke!"

No doubt, I thought, probably in the brawls which punctuated the evenings at Skeeter's. On a rope behind the bar, a baseball bat with the word PEACEMAKER burned into the wood told me that no one ever called the sheriff for assistance when the customers misbehaved. I suspected the bartender used it to subdue the last drunk standing before he dragged the incapacitated out the door and rifled their pockets for soiled, wadded bills.

Raymond coaxed two more rounds out of him.

"Does Mr. Skeeter know you insult your customers by calling them peckerheads and all?" Raymond asked.

"I'm Skeeter peckerhead."

Mr. Skeeter withdrew when one of his alcoholics came over and waved a $20 bill at him. Together, they left for the parking lot. As he passed us, he locked his eyes on me so hard I felt guilty for everything I ever did. Raymond leaned into me. "Chapter 2: We Make A Friend."

Before I could fully appreciate Raymond's wit, we were disturbed by a howl which I can only describe as the sound I would imagine a cat would make if you stabbed it with a stiletto. We turned as Dolly Parton burst into song:

"Wooooooomannnnnnn!!!! Love yur mannnnnnnn!!!

"He neeeeeeddss yore lovinnnnnnn!!!"

She'd seized the Karaoke machine and was belting out a local favorite because all the drunken animal molesters began clapping and hooting.

"Paint up theeeeemmmmm lipsssssss!!!

"Wiggle theeeeemmmmm hippssssssss!!"

Her breasts, which were fighting each other to be the first to leap out of her blouse, flew about with the enthusiasm of her musical delivery; sometimes in opposite directions.

"You think them titties are real?" Raymond asked over

the noise made by the patrons of the arts who were stamping their feet and clapping their hands.

"How did you find this place?" I asked.

"I got connections," he said, leaving me to wonder what kind of connections a guy like Raymond would have in the backwoods of a backwoods county.

Having exhausted her repertoire and being enticed with a beer and a cigarette Dolly Parton stumbled off the stage and into the recliner while her admirers gathered round for conversation. "Howdy fellers!" she said and inhaled a bottle of beer.

"You clowns come in here to drink or moon over our entertainers?" the bartender snarled.

"You're talking to a member of our nation's fighting forces," Raymond said, and pointed to me. "He's just back from Afghanistan."

"Yeah," Skeeter snorted. "He looks just dumb enough to volunteer to get his ass shot off for some tomfool reason that don't mean beans to nobody."

I probably should have said something since it was me that he was insulting, but the truth is, considering the state the country is in, he might have been right, and I might just be that dumb. Anyway, I quit caring about all that back somewhere in a filthy patch of sand I never learned the name of where I saw those things I won't ever tell to anybody. I was one of the lucky ones, and knowing that I was truly lucky was good enough, so I satisfied myself with that sobering consolation.

But Raymond didn't let it go. The beer relaxed his inhibitions, and he felt frisky.

"Maybe we ought to take our trade elsewhere."

"Sure, big spender. You can leave when you pay the cover charge." Mr. Skeeter grinned and put his hands on the edge of the bar.

"Cover charge?"

"You heard me."

"How much?"

"$20 bucks," Mr. Skeeter said. "Each."

"Cover charge for what?"

"The evening's entertainment," he nodded toward Dolly Parton who had passed out in the recliner.

"That drunk chick?" Raymond asked. "You call that singing?"

"That's my wife, peckerhead." Mr. Skeeter shouted like he'd been waiting all evening to start something and had decided now was the time.

The room, which had once been raucous with the sound of barnyard humor and the phlegmatic, cackling laughter that goes along with it grew quiet. Out of the corner of my eye I saw and felt everybody taking a break from guzzling beer, jacking their jaws, belching and farting to watch.

Some guy gets up, about five foot tall, with greasy hair and a snowfall of dandruff on the shoulders of his cowboy shirt, the kind of guy who would be nicknamed Wormy or Half Pint, and he points to us with a dip of his bottle and says, "These guys givin' you any trouble Skeeter?" He says it like he'll take care of things if just given the word.

"Nothing I can't handle," Mr. Skeeter says and nods to Wormy in a way that told him to go away and have a seat. He did.

"$40 bucks peckerheads."

"Are these guys paying your cover charge?" Raymond asked, his arm sweeping toward the barnyard.

This caused much merriment among the peasantry, and Raymond took the opportunity to whisper, "We'll escape in the confusion". Before I could ask "what confusion?" he shouted: "We're so glad we're entertaining to a bunch of animal molesting hillbillies what ain't got sense enough to pour piss out of a boot!" That roused them up, and Mr. Skeeter went for his ball bat with my beer bottle flying close behind his head. "Scram!" Raymond shouted as more bottles got thrown. Lawn chairs screeched on concrete and card tables collapsed as drunks lurched from their seats and we shoved them down onto the drunks still struggling to get up, tearing through that crowd like linebackers charging out of the backfield against a team of nursing home residents. They went down hard, and we went out the door.

The accident part came next.

Over my shoulder, I saw a flurry of arms and legs spurt out the doorway and into the parking lot.

Raymond dropped the keys while rummaging his pockets on the run, and they slid under the Caddy. At the passenger door, I watched the storm of drunken ferocity coming toward us while Raymond dropped to his knees and began searching under the car. A calm came over me, and I clinched my fists and started to rejoin Raymond to meet our pursuers together, but he popped up with the keys.

Raymond twisted the keys and the Caddy roared as people began beating on the windows and fenders. He stood up on the accelerator jamming it down on the floor, and in a gravel parking lot, the laws of dynamic physics being what they are, when he tried to spin the two-ton mass of steel around in the direction of the highway we just kept on spinning in a big swirl, stirring up our own gravel dust-infused tornado and shooting gravel the size of chicken eggs out behind us in fan like a rooster tail, hitting cars and trucks and anybody dumb enough to be chasing us on foot while Raymond laughed like a hyena and shouted "Hang on buddy!"

And I was hanging on with my feet smashed into the floorboard, my hands braced up against the roof and my body thrust back in the seat by the G-forces pressing in on me like I was an astronaut and the big booster rocket was kicking in.

"Good Gawd A'Mighty!" somebody shouted.

"Head 'em up there!" someone else yelled.

We came out of the spin, headed toward and into the brick-o-block beer cave at about 75 mph.

Brick-o-block flew through the air like one of those computer screen savers that has stars or bubbles flying at you. There were at least two blocks sitting on the hood when we fully re-entered the premises. Those drunks who had decided to sit out on beating us up now leapt from their seats and dove away from the Caddy like flying fish before a speedboat as we began pushing up an avalanche of aluminum chairs and card tables like a rampaging bulldozer at a weekend flea market.

Just before we hit the wall on the other side of the small room, I shouted: "Anybody hurt?!" I thought it would sound good at our manslaughter trial when I testified from the witness stand in my defense to show I really cared about the well-being of my fellow man, even those who were drunks, wife beaters and animal rapers.

The tenor of all the shouts and screams we heard were more of the "we-will-kill-you" genre rather than the "I've been crushed by a car and am dying" variety. I took some solace in that.

"Let's get the hell out of here," Raymond shouted.

"You think?!" I thought he was going to pitch it into reverse, but instead, he gunned it and we exited through the back wall as we had entered the front. We landed on five or six trash cans out back and rolled around on them before the car crushed them flat, and we were able to resume our forward movement. Feral cats leapt away from us, suspended momentarily in air with all four legs outstretched as they tried to stay out from under the Caddy's screaming wheels, although that sound could have been the terrified screaming of wild cats.

"Didn't use enough concrete on them walls if you ask me," Raymond shouted as he hopped the car up onto the highway.

We drove off with me tossing bricks, trash and assorted construction debris out of the car as the road unfolded before us shiny and black as a cobalt ribbon in the moonlight.

We'd lost the glass from the car windows at Skeeter's, and the wind was blowing through the car like a hurricane. The Corps had taken all of my hair, but Raymond's was blown backwards over his head so that it waved behind him like a tattered flag.

"You think I hurt anybody back there?!" The wind snatched Raymond's words out of his mouth, but I heard enough to shout back, "No more than they would've been hurt anyway on a Friday night at Skeeter's!"

"You think I'm going to jail?!"

"We're underage and involving the law is the last thing a place like Skeeter's wants."

"Well, I had a good time," Raymond announced. "… except for the disagreement there at the end."

I had to admit, we'd done a lot of living in just a couple of hours.

"I got a proposition for you," Raymond shouted at me. "You're gonna love this."

I looked at him like "I heard you, but I'm not sure I want to listen to you. I might, though, because I don't have anything better to do."

"It's about Elvis owning this car."

ABOUT THE AUTHOR

Michael Gigandet is a retired lawyer in Tennessee. His stories have appeared in Bending Genres, Quarencia Press, Great Weather for Media, Palm Sized Press, Syncopation Literary Journal and The Hong Kong Literary Journal. He is being nominated for a Pushcart Prize this year. His published stories are available here http://michaelgigandet.com. He administers a music page on Twitter/X at @motobec810

8

GALAGA DREAMS. A STORY
BY RAY VAN HORN, JR.

1982.

She was wearing Calvin Klein, though I was more of a Jordache guy. Not that it mattered. Holly Kolakowski could make bargain rack Levi dungarees a denim billboard of sin the way she rocked her lean hips and trim ass, thrusting her crotch at video game machines. She conquered them like older ladies did with men.

Playing Galaga and Time Pilot, Holly was clothed in amateur porn when she had her fist clenched upon a joystick and her right-ward middle three fingers pounding fire buttons. She'd made Galaga her bitch and seldom few got their turns if she'd claimed the alien shooting game first.

Holly Kolakowski was hardly my crush. That was Jeannie Maser, who didn't know I existed, even having three classes together.

Holly was dropping the equivalent of a hate fuck upon the Dig Dug machine, of all low-stress games. Her toned buttocks were clenching and grinding, putting on a hell of a show for the lookee-loos.

By the time I said what I had to say to Holly, the show would be over.

One of us would be gone for good.

Space Port was popping tonight, for a Thursday. The neon piping broke into the dimly lit fugue of the arcade, reminding me of Tron. The movie, of course, since the way-too-easy game had lain like a wet fart without the roast to check oneself. The Tron machine stood there right now, unwanted, like a lone, greasy spaz at Prom Night.

The orchestra of electric mayhem in the way of bleeps, doops, zaps and artificial detonation was supplemented by jangles of the dollar changer machines and Journey's "Don't Stop Believin'" waxing overhead. The song had already become a cliché for me.

The murkiest part of Space Port, between other shunned games like Pengo and Xevious was a crevice just enough for two people to squeeze into. Amongst us kids, it was called "The Makeout Zone." Right now, occupied by Keith Shaw and Valerie Spinelli. They were going at it hot, to the point Keith went for the hooter honk in plain view and Valerie didn't check him for it.

"Get bent," Valerie snarled at me as I lingered too long watching them.

"The looks of things, I'm not the one getting bent tonight," I sent back with the same smartass tongue my parents warned would get my duff kicked one day. Val snickered at my jibe. Kevin flipped me off.

Holly was hammering the pump action button on Dig Dug so hard I'm surprised she didn't sprain her wrist. Not fast enough, however, as she was gobbled by one of those weird, bloated ghost things wearing what looked like ski goggles.

Game over.

"Holly," I said, feeling provocation rise inside my throat.

"The hell do you want, Ricky Lowe?" she sassed with a whirl from the machine. "Got a quarter? I'm out."

"No," I said flatly, a total lie since I still had seventy-five cents inside my pocket.

"Then take a hike, already," she said with more dismissal than Rhett Butler's brutal parting shot to Scarlett O'Hara.

"I just want you to know, Holly," I said, looking into hazel eyes now darting around nervously. Murderer's eyes. "I know what you did."

"Say what?" she hissed, taking a step away from me.

I took the same step, blocking her path.

"I know."

"You don't know shit," she growled, guilt flashing across her face. The gleam of an unoccupied Missile Command machine accented her culpability. "Whatever it is you think I did."

"Two words for you," I said confidently, again stepping into Holly's path.

"Out of my way, Ricky, before I kill you," she fumed, clenching both fists.

Now I had her.

"Like you did to Wayne Reynolds. Well, that was six words, but whatever."

If a girl could go paler than a winter whiteout, that's how Holly looked, even with aquamarine, yellow and ultraviolet flushes slashing her liable face.

It was a wild card play, but last night my curiosity was up. I'd found a watermelon Bubblicious gum wrapper at the crime scene where Wayne Reynolds' brains had been bashed out with a hammer. No prints detected. Holly'd had enough savvy to wear gloves.

Wayne once bragged to me in the locker room he'd kissed Holly underneath the visiting side bleachers on the football field. He'd said her breath was "rancid from that stupid watermelon gum."

Why Holly had killed Wayne, I didn't know.

All I do know is the following morning, the cops had their girl.

ABOUT THE AUTHOR

Ray Van Horn, Jr. is the author of

Bringing in the Creeps, Behind the Shadows, Coming of Rage and Revolution Calling.

Ray is a contributing writer for The Metal Hall of Fame and he has covered music and film for outlets such as Blabbermouth, AMP, Pit, Dee Snider's House of Hair, Music Dish, DVD Review, Horror News.net, Fangoria Musick, Hails & Horns, Metal Maniacs, Noisecreep and many others.

Ray was an NHL game analyst for The Hockey Nut. Ray was a runner-up finalist in Alfred Hitchcock Mystery Magazine's "Mysterious Photograph" contest.

His work has appeared in Rue Morgue, Eternal Haunted Summer, Punk Noir, Atomic Flyswatter, Horror Tree, Cyber Age Adventures, Flash in a Flash, The Rubbertop Review, Story Bytes, Quantum Muse and New Noise, plus the anthologies Dread Mondays, Horror A-Z: X, Axes of Evil and Axes of Evil II.

9

NOTHING LEFT UNSAID. A STORY BY LAURA LEARY

Claudia opened one eye. A bar of purple-flecked soap partially blocked her vision. Confusion settling over her like a prickly wool blanket, she immediately understood that something was gravely wrong.

Normally, awakening to the rhythmic slap of water advancing and retreating in an endless dance of dark blue waves along the Maine shoreline, Claudia stubbornly shut her eyes, desperate to cling to the last wisps of her dream. Conjuring a vivid seaside vision, she could feel warm water licking her earlobe, smelling strangely of lavender and eerily out of context.

"Damn it," she muttered, instantly choking on a mouthful of soapy water. "What the hell?" she spat out for good measure with a satisfied grin.

At age 85, swearing was her new pleasure. And despite her concerning circumstances, Claudia grinned, imagining her caregiver, Mabel, muttering a blessing and pleading with the angels every time Claudia cursed. Just imagining it made her laugh with satisfaction.

Immediately, a sharp stab of pain erupted, like an ice pick punching a hole in her side, lodging its pointed blade deep in her lung. Struggling to catch her breath, Claudia realized not only that she was naked, but her brittle body was sprawled between the shower floor and the bathroom rug.

Surveying her surroundings, Claudia recalled her petulant desire for a warm shower before bed. She loved the blissful pleasure of the hot needles of water sluicing across her back and legs. Not even a glass of expensive sherry could match it. So, she had snuck out of bed tonight and stepped into the warm spray despite Mabel's admonishment before leaving for the night.

"Ms. Claudia, I bathed you yesterday," Mabel scolded in her deep New Orleans drawl. "Hot showers don't help your eczema, and I'm always worried you're going to fall without my help. I don't have time for this right now. It's my one free night to watch the harbor fireworks."

"For Christ's sake," Claudia argued, "I pay you a fortune to attend to me, and I'm not above firing you!"

"Your daughter Rebecca pays me, and she's the only one who can fire me," Mabel spat back, grinning a gap-tooth smile at the empty threat and enjoying their harmless sniping.

"If you ever talked to her, you'd know she thinks I treat you like a queen," Mabel said before gently smoothing Claudia's hair off her forehead and tucking the down blanket tighter around her slight frame.

Stung by this truth, Claudia reflected on her previous fall twelve months ago. Her attempt to reach a box of holiday ornaments resulted in a badly broken arm. But worse yet, she woke up confused and sore as Rebecca woodenly sat vigil next to her hospital bed.

"Mother, you cannot manage without help, and I can't provide daily care when I live two hours away. We're hiring Mabel, and that's the end of it," Rebecca curtly explained.

As part of the caregiver agreement, Mabel left Claudia alone one night each month. She would tuck Claudia into bed and drape an emergency call button around her neck before heading out to enjoy a night alone.

"I'm never going to use that goddamn button," Claudia groused. "You'll find me flat out dead on the floor before I grab for that." But tonight, Claudia began to regret her hubris.

Her recent move to mid-coast Maine was a boondoggle if Claudia admitted the truth. But she had come to this glorious place for 40 years, and she would be damned if her advancing age would limit her lifestyle. Yet, she was becoming exceedingly clumsy and lost her balance easily.

Worse were the periods of forgetfulness as her memory faded in and out. And her diminishing mental sharpness was occurring far more quickly than her doctors predicted.

"Bastards!" she shouted to the empty bathroom, satisfied by the slight echo that bounced back from the clean white walls and delighted by her use of yet another profanity.

Doctors were her sworn enemies, with their quiet evaluations and hastily scribbled but inaccessible notes. Recently, she snuck a furtive glance at her chart when her doctor turned away. Her blood turning to ice, she read the diagnoses of "likely Alzheimer's" and "progressive and rapid mental deterioration."

With Mabel not returning until the morning and in increasing pain, Claudia began to realize her injuries were far more serious than she initially thought. The most pressing issue was getting out of the relentless shower spray, now quickly turning cold. But her body refused to respond. Tonight, her legs no longer moved under her control. Her arms worked just fine, but she could not stand, let alone walk. With a herculean effort, Claudia slowly propped herself on her forearms and pulled her limp and useless body across the zero-edge shower pan like a decrepit soldier in a mud pit crawl.

"Ancient AF Women – Uncle Sam Still Wants You!" Claudia muttered under her breath, conjuring an imaginary Army recruitment poster. Sighing, she said a silent thank-you for the plush area rug she insisted on installing to cover the cold tile.

"A hundred dollars a square foot for fancy French tiles,

only to cover them with a cheap-ass rug?" Mabel chastised. "Rich people got no damn sense."

Shivering from the exertion and cold, Claudia saw a rapidly growing dark purple bruise now accompanying the pain in her side. Propping herself against the white shaker cabinets in a half-slumping pose and gritting her teeth, Claudia tugged at the terry cloth robe hanging above her head. After several tries and ultimately ripping off the fabric loop, she slipped her arms backward through the sleeves, covering her body as much as possible and finally stopping her shivering.

"Shit!" Claudia spoke to no one in particular, feeling slightly less buoyed than usual by her sailor's mouth. Surveying the scene, she grimaced, seeing her emergency call button uselessly dangling from the towel bar across the room, completely out of reach unless she miraculously sprouted wings. Worse yet, her washrag had lodged itself over the drain, slowly creating an expanding water dam on the floor as the shower continued to run.

Claudia sighed heavily, considering how Rebecca would react once Mabel relayed this recent catastrophe. Ordinarily, a child might be thankful that their mother survived the ordeal with nothing more than a broken rib or two and a bruised ego. However, her relationship with Rebecca did not mirror the regular loving connection between typical parents and children.

"If you fall again, you'll force my hand," Rebecca sternly conveyed during their last phone call a year ago. "I will have no choice but to put you in a nursing home. There is simply no other option."

"There are always other options," Claudia bristled at the

ultimatum. "You just don't want to consider them. So instead, you'll shove me into a home and warehouse me there until I die! After all the attention and care I gave to you when you were growing up?"

"You mean all the care my nannies provided and the attention of bullies I got at the boarding schools that destroyed the last shreds of my adolescence?" Rebecca scoffed.

"Those schools were the best that money could buy. Ivy League prep, every one of them," snapped Claudia.

"Well, Mother, you know what they say about karma. But don't worry, I'll find the best facility that your money can buy. And I'll hold my breath waiting for any appreciation," Rebecca sarcastically retorted and hung up without a goodbye. They had not spoken again.

Sadly, Claudia was unsurprised by the outburst. Their relationship consisted of decades of disappointment and massive communication failures. And lately, in her few clear-headed moments, she considered that her unrealistic expectations and short-tempered bouts of criticism played a role in their estranged relationship.

Closing her eyes and drifting back into her memories, Claudia recalled the sunlit days of her childhood. Her southern-belle mother called her an "unholy terror," as Claudia constantly found herself getting into every possible type of mischief. But her father loved her antics and encouraged her to defy the conventional debutante expectations. And she had done just that by landing a scholarship to attend Northeastern University, making her father beam with pride. Law school and an offer to join a prestigious Boston firm a few years later quickly propelled

Claudia into the inner circles of the corporate elite on Fleet Street.

"You like my brilliant mind and audacious legal strategies, but you love that I make you millions!" Claudia would crow to the senior partners. In turn, they made her smug, pretentious and pompous.

"Bitch," the junior associates called Claudia in those early years. Not flattering, but probably true. At the time, she wore it like a badge of honor, convincing herself it was a term of endearment. However, she didn't miss the irony when she fell for a hot-shot attorney who was the "male version" of herself, that the same adoring junior associates reverently referred to him as a "baller."

"Asshole," she muttered under her breath at the recollection. A whirlwind romance ensued, and they married in Wellesley, honeymooned in Florence, and dutifully produced Rebecca in a year. Unsurprisingly, her master-of-the-universe husband was cheating on her within six months. Even worse, the little slut he chose embodied everything Claudia did not. A simpering graduate from Choate who pledged to serve him shaken martinis, ignore the late hours he kept at the office (likely screwing his paralegal), and dutifully chair the local garden club. Claudia's marriage ended spectacularly upon this discovery, with a blowout in front of the country club elite, resulting in several shattered bottles of Moët and Chandon and her husband's new golf cart submerged in a pond off the 6th fairway.

"I'll never again lose my independence," Claudia would insist to her close female friends. "There's not a chance that another man will control my life. I just want to forget everything about our marriage!"

"But even though I despise him, I do love Rebecca; I just have difficulty showing it. She's so quiet and I can't understand her for the life of me," Claudia would protest to her girlfriends.

"It's just odd that she never wants to play with other children. All she does is tuck herself under the staircase and read or play with her puppy. She'll never go anywhere in life if she keeps this up." Claudia lamented.

Suddenly eyeing her daughter peeking around a corner, she would implore her, "Oh, Rebecca! Come here and give me a kiss!" Dutifully, Rebecca would brush her lips against her mother's powdered cheek and quickly shrink away as if the maternal contact stung like a charged third rail.

As the past faded out, Claudia once again opened her eyes to the harsh glare of the bathroom lights. Contemplating their last phone call that ended so spectacularly, she wondered if there might be a kernel of truth behind Rebecca's anger. Had she replaced hugs and kisses with showers of material possessions and a multitude of nannies to provide what she could not easily show her daughter? After all this time, Rebecca must know that Claudia truly loved her… but what if she didn't?

Trapped on the floor in her bathroom but feeling more lucid than she had in months, Claudia noted the dark pool of blood on her left side was now accompanied by an odd crackling each time she took a breath. She desperately needed a distraction to help her ignore the pain and the bizarre feeling taking over her body.

"I can't do a goddamn thing!" Claudia whispered, an ounce of fear creeping into her usually confident demeanor.

Looking around for options to distract her, she saw her makeup bag within reach on the upholstered vanity stool. Alongside lay the spiral notebook and pen used by Mabel to track Claudia's daily water intake, blood pressure, and oxygen levels. Not that those details would do any good if Claudia tragically died of an internal hemorrhage or froze to death on the floor. It figured that when her mind felt sharp as a razor, naturally, her body picked this occasion to fail her.

Claudia began ripping out every page of data from the little notebook that recorded the dreary death march of her body. This little journal synthesized her life into the most mundane and insignificant details. Where was the evidence of the spontaneous woman who would catch a flight from Boston and be in New York by dinner? Or the theater patroness who had seen every Tony Award-winning musical on Broadway since 1950?

Claudia's life used to be big and extravagant. Her friends, too numerous to count, vied for invitations to her famous dinner parties, golf outings or champagne-soaked summer regattas at the Boston Yacht Club. Or at least they used to. But over the years, that life of spontaneity and fun became quiet and dull. Long-time friends jetted to Florida, fell in love with the tropical warmth and did not return.

Despite living only two hours apart, Claudia rarely visited Rebecca's home in New Hampshire. But with the dawning of the holiday tomorrow, Claudia perked up at writing a short letter to Rebecca and ringing in the New Year with a clean slate. Mabel could mail it in the morning, and if everything went according to plan, Rebecca might soften up and agree to meet for a long-overdue brunch.

The little spiral notebook held twenty blue-lined pages with all but the last four filled on both sides. Ripping out the last pages of her medical stats with a flourish, she wadded each offensive sheet into small balls and shot them at the wicker basket across the room. Only three found their mark. Sighing at the abysmal success rate, she surveyed the contents of the open makeup bag, as a well-used tube of Elizabeth Arden lipstick caught her eye.

"Why do you insist on painting your old, wrinkled face that hooker color?" Mabel often quipped to Claudia.

Claudia would snap back, "For your information, Victory Red is the most iconic lip color ever made, you silly fool!"

Sighing dramatically, Mabel ultimately took the lip color and would gently apply it to Claudia's thinning lips, eliciting a smile of delight as Claudia gazed into the mirror. "There you go, Ms. Claudia," Mabel would softly say, "Now you're ready to meet the Queen."

Claudia suddenly remembered the story behind her signature lip color. As a little girl, Rebecca begged her to tell it, watching mesmerized as Claudia painted her lips the vibrant shade. Picking up the pen, she smiled and slowly began to write the familiar tale to her daughter in a shaky scrawl.

"Dear Rebecca,

I found myself with extra time on my hands today and wanted to dash off a quick letter to my favorite daughter. Maybe I am becoming sentimental in my old age, but you have been on my mind lately. And don't fret, I'm doing quite well and safely ensconced in bed while Mabel enjoys her night off. That should allay your concerns and end our silly discussion of a nursing home, once and for all."

Claudia figured a little white lie for the benefit of her overly worrisome daughter could not possibly send her to hell tonight. Glancing at the once insignificant puddle of water, now spreading halfway across the rug, she decided that the potential of drowning remained a tiny possibility, and as such, she could justify a little literary license.

"Do you remember when I would tell you the story of my Victory Red lip color? It remains one of my favorite memories. You would sit beside me at my vanity and watch me fill in my lips. I recall your beautiful eyes shining in the mirror – eyes that perfectly matched my periwinkle color, ringed with the dark lashes of your ~~philandering~~ father – (oops, sorry sweetheart, no eraser.)

In the 1940s, women believed that "beauty was your duty." The military asked Elizabeth Arden to create a lipstick specifically designed for women in service. It was a bright, dazzling red that perfectly matched the piping on women's military uniforms. It symbolized success and confidence, worn by brave women who helped turn the tide of the war. Confident in an ultimate victory, it was worn by millions of women worldwide who embodied tremendous strength and perseverance. It still reminds me of you."

Claudia paused, wondering if she sounded preachy or overbearing. No, she didn't think so. She simply recalled the tale she spun around her daughter during the few moments each day that they would sit quietly together.

"Goodbye, darling, I'll be back in the morning!"

Claudia would sing out as she grabbed her fur coat from the nanny and whisked out the door through a mist of perfume.

But occasionally, she would glance back at Rebecca and see a glistening of tears in her eyes. Claudia did not dwell on those emotions. Rebecca's sad and pleading look made her irritable and unbearably uncomfortable. After all, she always returned from each event just as she promised. But tonight, decades later and covered in a damp robe on the bathroom floor, Claudia suddenly saw the scene through the eyes of her young daughter.

"Fuck," she whispered as her eyes filled with hot, stinging tears.

And there it was…the painfully honest, band-aid-ripping truth that recently niggled around the corners of her mind, now exploding with crystal clear precision. Each of the blocks seemed to fall into place with deafening clarity. Claudia's desire to protect her heart from the hurt of a failed marriage had ultimately failed her only child. Claudia realized she had spent her days living for the next deal, project, or black-tie event. She never enjoyed the present, and worse yet, she built up an impenetrable wall around herself. Resenting the past and coveting the future, Claudia forgot the fragile feelings of her precious daughter.

Watching the slowly spreading puddle of water begin licking her ankle, Claudia finally started to write earnestly, pouring out her heart like a dam released. The sentences flew out of her fingers, filling the last few remaining notebook pages with apologies, requests for forgiveness and unconstrained words of love. She wrote until the carpet around her became soaked with water, and her hand cramped in protest.

"Bloody hell!" Claudia shouted, shaking the now-empty blue pen before hurling it across the room and searching the makeup bag for an option to finalize the letter.

Sighing with relief, Claudia found a whittled-down waterproof eyebrow liner. Picking up the remaining tiny nub, she turned to the final page of the little notebook with a sense of peace. After two sentences, the liner broke, ultimately bringing her letter to its final conclusion. Satisfied nonetheless, Claudia sealed her final words by drawing a massive heart in Victory Red.

IN the dimly lit station lobby, Rebecca watched the officer return to the glass window behind the sterile viewing room where she had stoically made the identification.

"We won't know for sure till the medical examiner finishes, but she probably threw a clot from the fall. Likely, she went quickly and didn't suffer," said the officer without making eye contact.

"Just a few forms to sign, and we can release her belongings to you," the robotic, grey-haired sergeant rasped. "Not much here except a little notebook. The paramedics grabbed it, but it might have got some water damage. She was holding it pretty tight."

Rebecca sighed and signed the forms. She picked up the plastic bag with the notebook and wordlessly walked away. That evening, with a glass of wine and the glowing logs of the fireplace warming her, she opened the bag to read the little notebook. Each wrinkled page was covered by streaks of wavy blue lines, trickling down to the bottom edge and disappearing. Page after page, each impossible to read.

On the last page, the writing finally became legible. It appeared to be written in a different type of ink with an indecipherable pinkish-red splotch at the bottom.

"Sweetheart, on these pages, I have told you everything I should have said a thousand times before. No matter what tomorrow brings, I can rest easy, knowing finally, there is nothing left unsaid…"

ABOUT THE AUTHOR

Laura is an emerging writer who lives, works, and plays in the beautiful state of Colorado.

She is a member of the Denver-based Lighthouse Writers community, and her previous work has been published in the San Antonio Review and The Umbrella Factory Magazine.

Her work can be found at www.learys-literature.com.

10

RISKING DELIGHT. A STORY
BY CHITRA GOPALAKRISHNAN

Truth, they say, is amoral. But what if serving your truth turns you into an immoral being?

I listen idly to the deep, resonant whoop of a solitary coucal and then to the throaty chorus of coucal calls that follow, each bird call starting when one ends. As I sit on grass that is warmish and dampened by freak autumn rains in September, I try to discern their feathered presences among trees in the pale ribbon of the evening light. I look for their glossy bluish-black plumages, their chestnut wings and their black, loose, long tails but they are so perfectly blended within the dense tree recesses that they remain hidden.

Sitting in my rectangular garden, which takes over the front of my cottage on the outskirts of New Delhi, with a line of heavenward-shooting trees running along each side and a copse of varied smaller shrubs on the inside, I get the feeling that it is the greenery around that is summoning me with its full tones.

As the leaves of the trees and the shrubs shimmer with the moisture of rain, I wonder what their heightened calls give notice of, what secrets they divulge. A part of the double-dealing cuckoo family, I believe ornithologists when they say, "these coucal calls are more about what they hide than what they say."

I understand their theatrical masquerades as I understand myself. Dissembling has been among my early survival skills. The first marker of my oddness. The other being my lonely pursuit of choices that lie outside the norm.

Let me start with the smoke screen and the peculiarities of my current profession in the here and now of my life. In my early thirties, I work in an intimate market, in the business of buying and selling secrets. Let me explain. I am hired by shocked, betrayed wives who find their husbands straying. As a 'mistress dispeller', which is my official designation, I befriend the mistress, woman to woman, invade her life, uncover her weakness or her many damaging weaknesses to the wife so as to break up the liaison

As I see it, I excel in my outlandish job, in the 'private intel space', as I call it, as no one knows better than me of the unbridled excitement of forbidden attachments. If I know how to nurture such connections, then I know as much about how to undo them with nonchalance. But more of my own earlier life of sensuality, when I unwind the tale of my past from my tale of my today, the life of my yesterday from the life of my today.

To a charming gossip columnist, Vidya Jain, whom I gave an 'in' into my world, I confessed, "I, unwittingly and to my bemusement, also break up a medley of marital peculiar orders and family arrangements that have come to be in our city's contemporaneity,"

Vidya, in her column, spoke of my innate sensibilities of a spy that aid me in my job. She said, "She has a keen sense of observation, a knack of idly engaging and finding common ground with anybody, the plusses of a natural liar (you really can't learn to lie as you will trip up sooner than later), a clandestine, street-wise ability to press the limits of rules and regulations to test how much she can get away with, an artist's (some would murmur a con artist) ability to talk her way out of trouble and a preparedness to be adaptive toward changing situations."

To this, she added, "She even uses technology with élan, her spy pen being her most useful aide memoir and infected phones her best spyware, a giveaway of all secrets on her cloned screens." She also put in what I reiterated in my talk with her. "I know with certainty that every application on the phone has a backdoor and that hacking tools are as easy to access as an Uber cab."

I, understandably, did not give her permission to use my name. But I must admit she is as much of a deadeye as I am and as able to extract information.

Samir Kaul, a freelance entertainment journalist, was not so charitable about my work. My client foolishly gave him my details, as she was riding on the wave of petulance and peevishness about her husband's infidelity. His piece said, "Her dishonourable undercover work is conducted using a footloose, freewheeling team – an assorted, deviant, group of hackers, fact-checkers, small-time sleuths, bush-league citizens with a kinship to the underworld, among many other such outliers – who roam Delhi's socio-economic borderline."

I had the piece, which identified me by name, squashed. An editor I knew tipped me of its scheduled date of appearance. I put my ragtag gang to work. They came up with lurid details of his life that I used to silence him and his piece. "Sweet revenge!" my team exulted.

So, in an odd sort of togetherness with my team, I have managed many a coup d'état. For the past four years, I have been carrying my burden of deception lightly, and, as a few who think they know what I do, say, with animation.

Only my psychiatrist has a whiff of my uneasiness, of how "I get divided within as I enter the troubled spaces of others and become part of the storm within their world" and how "the bizarre untruths and dubious acts make me unsure of the condition of my being, my inner core."

What dragged me to her couch a month ago with this baneful job were the beginnings of small fidgets of anxiety in my mind that worked themselves up into a lather of fretfulness. I now suffer from a permanent sense of inner discomfort and unease, impulses that are new to me. My old avatar was one of infinite self-assuredness. But, as I said earlier, more of that when I tell you of my past cocksureness.

Inclined, as a rule, towards guardedness, a dislike of having to share my private predicaments and given the nature of my job that calls for me not to be loose-lipped, it took me a long to reveal bits of myself to her.

As I was advised, full disclosure if I wanted to heal, I coerced myself to admit more than I wished. "Until now, I have had no qualms about the shape and order of my inner being," I said, "as manipulating situations and people gets me what I want. As it is the nature of fire to burn, it is my nature to hide what I am."

I suspect knowing who I am as opposed to who I appear to be disconcerted her. I also suspect that she, who was to render no judgment, did not have kind words for me in her copious assessment notes. As it was only her medicines, not she, who could soothe me somewhat, I discontinued my visits very soon.

Take my last assignment for Leela Sahani as a test case of what I do for a living and as a kind of explanation for my being in this lady's lair. Leela came to my office on a cold, foggy morning, in ire, determined "to chargrill her husband's lover into juicy smokiness". "Stop at nothing to uncover the truth of my husband's carousals," she instructed me. "Spy, catfish, break security codes, procure bank records under false claims, read personal correspondences, keep tabs on gifts, install spy cameras and eavesdrop in all manner of speaking. Do what it takes," she ordered.

In my world, where it is lived with a lot of screens and technology, I did most of what she asked for and some more on the ground with the help of my unholy team. My most invasive technique was to intimately befriend the young, radiantly voluptuous Ria Mathur, the 'other' woman, feigning similar passions and reciprocal altruism.

I went about it with the thoroughness of a method actor, by 'accidentally' bumping into her and starting an animated conversation that continued as banter for months on our cell phones, where we glittered on thus. I, in my contrarian, puckishly charismatic way, and, she, in her typical, abrasive, unrestrained, lippy, narcissistic Delhi way, coating her tongue with an unbearably coarse accent each time she spoke to me. She believed I found her immoderately charming.

She bargained her way into my affections and onto what she called my "classy way of life," buying sweaters for our iPhone (her iPhone was gifted by Leela's husband), Guci bags (as she could not afford the missing c in the name) and oily edibles, all of which found its way into my bin. I threw some baubles in her direction.

Our relationship almost took on the contours of an all-absorbing romance. She was hyper-verbal about everything in her life. "I love gol gappas (round, hollow, deep-fried crisp crepes filled with a mixture of flavoured water) and could eat it for breakfast, lunch and dinner." (Yikes!!) "My Pomeranian Pinky is my soul mate." (A breed that is an apology for a dog, if you ask me) "My boss loves my button nose and to peek at my cleavage." "My family is very strict and I am terrified of my brothers and father, but otherwise, I never dodge fights, hold my tongue or mind the rules with anyone."

She mistook my attentive listening for empathy.

Her candour about her boozy, seductive liaisons with Neel, Leela's husband, was equally cloying in its details. "I was so open and mast (flamboyant) while his responses were dara hua (scared and tentative). I love the way I melt in my insides like a maum (candle) in the heat of his mohhabat (passion)and the nasha (intoxication)of his tone when he calls me his jaan (life)."

I began to dread her phone calls, their clichéd dreariness and the sheer triteness of her conversations.

It took me no time with my dark art to know her vulnerability. You guessed right, it was as banal as money. I turned in her details and the jigsaw of my team's findings to Leela, who instantly bartered money in lieu of her soiled husband.

Of course, my tidbits on Ria's family life helped. Leela told me, "I fisted Ria and my husband's romance in the stomach, once for all, by threatening to tell of the affair to her family of three giant-looking brothers and I-can-give-complex-to-a-rhino kind of father. I said to her, This is my one-time payment to you and I want you to never contact my husband."

The outing of infidelity is rarely simple or dignified. The exposed are utterly unshelled, which is what happened to Ria and Neel. While I, in my perfect disguise, got to keep my camouflage as armour. They never knew the leak came from me, a fact that holds for all the cases I have handled so far.

I was, however, not completely exempt from downsides. I had to continue to hear Ria's inane chatter and despairing wails of being discovered for some more time to keep my work's tell-tale features hidden. For 'plausible deniability of involvement', as we call it in our professional parlance. And, two, I had to face up to the fact that my head was no longer as steady, no longer as inured to the risks and the insanity of my profession, its masterful puppetry of plying and pulling of others' life strings. Just to be clear, I was not bothered by my subterfuges being uncovered. My insecurity arose from my hair-trigger paranoia of my psychological stability. I was assailed by a sense of losing myself, of having gone too far down the void of a rabbit hole, of not being in control of my life and my person, something very unfamiliar and frightening for me. I would never have believed such a thing probable in my life when in my twenties and would have laughed in anyone's face if they said I would be seeing a shrink in my life.

I have always found camouflage to be a wonderful thing as I am sure you have inferred by now. My seeming to be someone else while concealing who I really am has been a captivating game for me since childhood. I have lived in my shadows of subterfuge for so long that my disguises are now a part of me. They have never felt wrong or dysfunctional, but fun like play-acting.

In my growing-up years, my father often worried about me growing up without a mother, the lack of her influence and anchoring. He would point me to a picture of the wheel in our drawing room, say that it should remind me of living my life from the centre. "When we live our life from the rim of the wheel, we focus on externals, what you can see with your eye or hear with your ear. Externals will never make you strong in your inner core," was something he repeated to me often.

Did he sense my secrecy and cover-ups even then? My little manipulations and the small contradictions in my stories? Was he worried that what he permitted could turn into what he promoted? A number of times, I felt in my bones that he seriously disapproved of my lack of a blood bond to him and my tenuous attachments to friends. His constant urging me to "grow more affection and altruism" confirmed his dim view of my lack of filial and fraternal fidelity.

Conflicts of my amoral outlook did register in my furrowed brows at a young age. At fourteen, to the confession priest in my school's church, I said, "Father, I worry about why moral perfection is not burrowed into my sense of the world. I do try time and again to lean towards goodness, but I fail." All he said was, "Mend your ways, child, find your path towards God." The holy water he gave me was supposed to help. It didn't.

Such urges simply died when I reached my twenties. The subterranean hum of my true nature became voluble by then, and I began to accept the freefall of my basic tendency. One that was to maximise my utility at the expense of others, sometimes even at the risk of bringing about negative outcomes in others' lives. At this point in my life, I came to a clear understanding that I have been involuntarily following my innate instincts all through my life and that I will continue to do so, as this is the only way I know how to be.

My elite life in New Delhi, ten years past the turn of the millennium, was, hence, an indulgence, unbound by any ideological mooring, one persuasion or another. I overheard one girl say of me, "She is simply interested in getting as much as she can for herself, her personal interest acting as her sharpest spur to action. She sees inventive dissembling in the guise of simple naiveté as a good way of getting by as being strategic in choosing when to cooperate." She was not wrong.

While at the campus in the northern part of the city, doing a post-graduate course in economics, I never bought into the argument that my economics professor would tout, "that it is in understanding the interests of others that we are able to fulfil our own." My counter was "attempting idealised perfectibility and equality in personal, political, economic and social spheres will always fail. The dark mirror of utopias, dystopias, will show up in fallen social experiments, stringent political regimes and controlling economic systems."

These beliefs may sound Machiavellian to some, but I never did read him at length at that point. My beliefs sprang from my own interpretations of the world around me. It surprised me then as it does now, that my old professor held on to human goodness while I ingested the meaning of utopia to be 'no place' both literally and metaphorically. And that I have always believed that disinterest in gathering personal resources is ideologically unhealthy.

So as I was saying, life in my twenties was a time of

riotous springtime joy. My diary note for this period says, "My life now is a seemingly eternal season of silk cotton fluff fluttering in a breath of wind. A time when 'adventure' is the ticket. A time when it feels beautiful to be in my body, when a golden heat flows skin-deep, vital and shining. A time to allow passion to take up space within my body's clear, effusive warmth, changing the balance, making ripples in the air that it passes through. A time to throw away the cultural scripts written for women."

It was easy for me with my erotic loveliness and with my umbrella shadow of luck and privilege to flit fast from liaison to liaison within New Delhi's gilt-edged, closed-in community. I went on thus compulsively and in secret for eight long years. As I sought transitory physical attachments and never emotional closeness that tended to feelings, my many past lovers were put one by one where they belonged, out of my life and in the past. As I saw that the simplicity and security of one partner was not for me, I cleared each of my lovers' residual impact quickly to reclaim my sexual sovereignty. For me, the idea of taking on inner pain in the name of love was needless torture. It never happened.

I don't think it was my attractiveness that particularly drew men to me. There were women with far more beauty and feminine mystique. I think what one of the men in my life said to me explains why men were drawn to me. "You send out subconscious scent signals that urge a sexual response." So I will go with my all-scented wanton woman body as the reason for my appeal and as the reason for why I unwound men.

It was one connection in particular that held me for a

very long. I note in my diary that it was "pulse-pounding, ardent, dangerous and disruptive." Dangerous and disruptive as, in our case, we were both married. It was no impediment, though, despite the watched and guarded nature of personal and social lives.

My diary entries for this period are uninhibited. "Our lust is on the loose. We taste the excitement of each other's lives and yearn for another thousand faraway possibilities. It is so exciting to carry on our furtive trysts with note messages tucked into bicycles, furtive calls through the day, midnight meetings and through the courting each other through poetry in well-modulated cadences."

"The folds of our sheets could tell stories of just how truly bad we are," we would often joke. Our affair was freighted with lies, secrets and ongoing deceptions that uncontained relationships like this need. We risked our delight as there was no license in my marriage or his to open up our experiences and connections to others. Or to reshape it in any way to our needs.

Thinking back, I realize I must have had holes in my conscience through all my many relationships post-marriage as it remained oddly innocent through all the illicit dangerousness. And my middle-class Indian background, that should have tethered me with moral chastity belts, not even allowing my fantasies to roam freely, failed in its reign-in.

The backlash to our lustful daredevilries arrived swiftly, once we got found out. His wife called me up to yell, "You rubbishy creature, how could you do this to me and my child? I can't think of another person in the whole world that I despise more than you. You have the morals of an alley cat and I will pray that you rot in hell in a sludge of substances." Her succession of emails was far more vitriolic and delivered a tirade of expletives. She threatened to inform my husband and ruin my life. She did. My marriage and my double life folded.

My life's deceptions were witnessed by all, and my personal stories were made public. I was made to map the extent of my misdemeanours. People, especially women, saw me as a "labyrinth of many unknown paths," and I let them live with their belief. I guess because it was true in many ways. I had to use indifference as a defence mechanism to counter my powerlessness. It is not as if I did not hurt from the inside, but the recognition of who I really am insulated me, made me understand that my adventuresome actions and decisions were in many ways ineludible.

In defence of my husband, I think he would have been able to handle "minor paltering's" but he could not cope with my "many flat out deceptions', as he termed them. Once my lover's wife outed our deception, many other women were emboldened to whisper to him "about how I turned my affections towards him to others."

And it is also not as if my husband did not try to understand me or my indiscretions. He did. But we were toppled over by another awkward trio that came to be – him, the counsellor, and me. We made efforts to cut through the complications and permanent barriers created, but failed. The counsellor felt my reasons for straying and staying were "delusive" and noted that I "felt no guilt that most others would feel when engaging in stuff like this, something hurtful to others."

Finally, my husband gave up, saying, "I think there is

nothing left to save. Now my entire idea of what the world is, and the truth of what is and isn't, feels like it is on a chopping board and that trust between us is a thing of the past. In fact, I am not certain we had trust to begin with."

I begged and I pleaded. It was ignominious. "Let's start afresh. I promise to be true to you. I will make up for the times I let you down," I beseeched. My moment of complete abasement came when I cried, "Where will I go if you leave me? I have nothing to fall back on. What will I do?"

He remained unmoved. Our marriage came to an end when I reached the age of thirty with one signature and two court hearings. It purged me of all my relationships and friendships.

Looking back, I see that I mostly observed my husband from under closed eyelids through our eight-year connection. All I can say is the mild warmth of my marriage at twenty-two years of age and his unrelenting gravity bored me, and I "could not be demure and domestic" as my mother-in-law curtly said in her first assessment of me when my father and she met to "marry me off", as they call the curious social engineering of arranged marriages.

I know all of this sounds like an easy summation of the situation or of why I was not as safe or knowledgeable as other women around. My arguments do lack introspection and show up my inability to face up to the crucial actions in my life as well as my casual, cruel displacement of an individual. But that is all I have as that is how I am.

Maybe I should have taken my dead aunt Renuka's notion of singlehood, as a desired way of life, seriously and fought with more intensity against being ambushed into marriage. She did, in her sickness, warn me when my father was pushing me into marriage. "Don't allow boldness of your aspirations to be bleached into a pastel of family expectations. I know you well and this is what will happen if you marry."

No one knows how a thing like a divorce will strike you before it comes to you. But one thing was certain: I brought on a dreadful reckoning over which I had no control. I reeled for months under an unfamiliar sense of insecurity and the harsh realization that I had no particular skills to make a living. The sniggers of those around who said "she will probably allure a whole organization now" cut to the bone. But at least I had a place to stay. My father, who passed on two years ago, erasing all records of my childhood, left behind a cottage on the outlying part of the city, from where I could make a new beginning.

In my thwarted life, I chose to be a mistress dispeller as it fell within my catchment area. I had never known it to be a thing until my marriage was spluttering and I heard whispers that my lover's wife had employed one to peel away my secrets. I don't know if she did. I do know a woman who sought to befriend me around the time of my last affair, and I did reciprocate, meeting her for an odd coffee or drink. I am not sure how much I said or whether she was why I got found out but the idea of the job description stuck in my head. Talk of life's ironies. It was my lover's wife, in a way, who set me up in this covert career.

So I live my life now with a job in the game of seduction, one that is heart-in-the-mouth, immediate and fierce in its gaze of the hidden, almost delivered from my societal shame. Or maybe not.

Today, is my new life, four years of age, with its changed balance in my role as a mistress dispeller, a liberation of sorts? A validation and affirmation of self-perceived abilities and a balm for injured self-esteem, as I see it? After all, I earn well, act as a relief worker for many distressed women, mask my own sexuality and keep my own life and its engagements denuded to a minimum, almost solitary, to erase my past waywardness.

Or is it really a doppelganger of an earlier existence, a double walk as it were, on the path of stealth and strategy? One with ethically, morally, and socially questionable attitudes and behaviours, as many say? After all, I do freely admit to the buzz I feel when codebreaking and the power I feel when I play god and wreak judgment on others' lives. This, even though I myself have indulged in such a lifestyle with abandon.

If pressed to find language about my current situation, I would say it is uncomfortable. My idea that the ground beneath me is solid, dependable, that I can build on it, that I can trust it to support me, is gone. The gaping hole in my mind, in my life, seems to mock the very idea of solid ground, of trustworthy geology.

I live off-course, in a state of doubtful uneasiness in my mind, rolling over peaks and troughs, splayed by them, and struggle to enter into a stable ground of belief about myself, my life. I look for the easygoing self-assurances of my life in my twenties, but they are nowhere to be found.

Is my strife within the beginning of consciousness?

I sit vertiginously atop a Ferris Wheel, the world

beneath me, wondering if the wheel wisdom of my father will work out answers for me.

Will it help me find my way back to things I can trust? Will it help me find my own floor? Should I adopt the wisdom wheel, its love and kindness, as my compass, as a way of coming to terms with myself, as my catharsis? Should I finally now accept my hubris in thinking I can control my life from its rim?

I need to find out fast before I lose myself. Before, I don't fit in my head at all.

ABOUT THE AUTHOR

Chitra Gopalakrishnan, a writer based in New Delhi, uses her writing to break firewalls between fiction and poetry, narratology and psychoanalysis, marginalia and manuscript, and treeism and capitalism. www.chitragopalakrishnan.com

11

ON DECK. A STORY BY WILLIAM GENSBURGER

She sat demure, blond hair straight down, mid-back length, smooth legs outstretched. Daniel didn't have a name for her yet, and was almost ready to settle on Karen-she looked like a Karen, pale skin, soft features, eyes made up to stand out, foundation hiding freckles, white and tight T-shirt, revealing curves. There was no doubt she was pretty, Daniel thought, and he had seen her every day for the four weeks he'd been coming to the skate park, watching from the air-conditioned comfort of his van parked a few feet away by the chain link that separated the skate park from the dirt parking area.

Karen had seen him, had gotten in the habit of looking his way every quarter hour or so, making eye contact for a second before looking elsewhere. She was seated on the grass in the shade thrown down by the pylons and concrete tracks of the spell BART system, oblivious to the trains scraping past, the sound blending with the grinding of skateboard lips onto metallic wrapping on concrete walls and steps.

Karen had two boys, Jason and Sam, whose real names he had heard when Karen had called them. Both boys were about 12 years old, and Karen was barely 30—she had lost her virginity young and lost the father moments after the pregnancy test glowed pink. There was no dad, no wedding ring, and she had the look of someone who had given up expecting a man to take her from the difficulty of single parenthood.

"You will not," Karen said loudly. Jason and Sam were laughing. Daniel couldn't determine why, but from his van, he smiled along with them-their tone was infectious. As if on cue, she looked his way, but only in passing.

The skate park was relatively new, a good addition for an otherwise generally drab Bay Area city in need of creative outlets for youth. The designers had done well, a series of bowls, half pipes, and steps with walls to keep all levels of skaters happy. The grassy area allowed a reprieve from the extreme California sun.

"I wouldn't let my boxers hang out like that," Jason teased. He was the more sensible of the two boys, slightly older, tall, almost six feet, lanky and gawky, yet with a certain grace to his movements when he skated. In a single movement, he lunged forward, dropping his board into a roll and casually stepping onto it, body leaning ever so slightly, arms by his side, palms facing back.

AT THE OTHER end of the park, his friends were taking a break, lined up orderly like sparrows on a telephone line or mosquito-shaped Harriet Jump jets stretched on the deck of an aircraft carrier waiting for the launch command.

Jason did a spin and landed on his ass, pants dropping, underwear showing. He pulled them up, accepted a few high-fives for the attempt, and assumed his place on deck. Friends didn't need words.

"Mom, come skate with me," Sam shouted. Karen smiled, shook her head, then looked at Daniel, who pretended not to have noticed. He envied her, enjoyed their visits. Sam reminded him of Alex, his own son, whom he had not seen for over two years. Such regrets are not correctable, Daniel told himself. Alex's mother had seen to that.

Karen had accepted Daniel as a daily fixture in a way beyond words. He had often thought about getting out of the car and actually talking to her, but he knew that he might never return if he did; he would learn that she was not as he had imagined, or worse, that she might not be so accepting of him, after all he was a man, alone, parked in a van at a kids' skate park; a definitive cause for concern. Of course, it was all open for interpretation as he had no way to know for sure what would happen short of actually finding out what she thought.

IT WAS ONLY when a skateboard sailed across the chain link fence and smashed into his hood, indenting a large section before falling to the floor, that the decision was made for him. He looked up to see Jason aghast, clutching at the fence in disbelief and, peripherally, Karen getting up and walking quickly toward him, only to realize that to reach him she would have to go all the way back and around, which she started to do.

Jason leaped over the fence and awkwardly landed in front of Daniel.

"I'm so sorry. I didn't mean to do that."

Daniel looked at the dent, large, visibly needing attention, and shrugged it off.

"It's fine, barely noticeable. Apology accepted." He forced a smile, watching Karen off to the side — she was out of the park now. "You do a good half-turn, but your landing needs work." He picked up Jason's skateboard and handed it back to him.

Jason stared in shock, expecting a tirade. "It's not nothing," he finally said, "it's huge. I'll have to pay for it to be fixed. My mom'll tell you..."

Daniel was shaking his head, backing off now to the car. He opened the door.

"It's nothing, really. Forget about it. I'm late for a meeting — have to go. Goodbye." And he got into the car, started it, backing away from the fence, from the park...from Karen, who, seeing him leaving, abruptly stopped. She was thirty feet away. She looked puzzled, then looked over at her son.

Daniel was gone, a cloud of dust from where he had backed roughly over the gravel. Jason walked to Karen.

"What happened?" she asked. "Didn't he need our insurance information?" He shrugged.

"He told me to forget it," Jason explained, "said it was nothing."

"Oh," she said. "That's odd. Did you at least get his name?"

Jason shook his head. "Maybe you should ask him tomorrow when he comes."

Karen smiled. Maybe she would.

But he did not return the next day. Karen arrived earlier than usual, hoping that he would be there. She had a good feeling about him, even though there seemed to be a lot of mystery surrounding him. She wondered why he was hiding, what could make him so uncomfortable. She felt awful that her son had dented his car, and she could not even give him insurance information, so she could pay for the repairs.

"You should talk to him, Mom," Jason said. "He'd understand. We know you like him." Sam nodded as though this had been some secret he had been protecting for months.

"Like him? I don't even know his name. How can I like him?"

Jason shrugged. "Why don't we make a name for him, that way we have something to call him?"

"Like what?"

Sam said, "I know – David. He looks like a David."

"David works," Jason said.

Karen smiled. "David, it is."

The following week, Karen began to be concerned. She had not seen David since the day of the accident. Now she sat waiting, watching each car pass as though he might at least drive by, even if he did not stop. Carefully, she scrutinized each face, in case he had used a different car. She didn't see him.

"Mom, I told you," Jason argued, "he didn't say anything except that I shouldn't worry about it."

"Was it a big dent?" Karen had asked again.

"It looked big, but he said it wasn't. I dunno, maybe it was there already."

"That doesn't make sense," she added. "I wonder why he didn't come back."

"I know that he seemed very nervous when he saw you coming closer. That's when he left."

"Me?" Karen did not understand why she should have made him nervous. "Did I look angry? Maybe he thought I would attack him?"

Sam began to laugh. "Mom, you don't attack people."

"I know, Sam, but what else could it be?"

"You like him, huh?" Sam asked her.

Karen smiled. She couldn't explain it. "Just a little. Maybe! He seems like he could be a nice man. I have a feeling that he is a father, but we haven't seen his children."

"Maybe he's divorced and doesn't have his kids. Like Dad."

Karen seemed angry at the mention of "Dad."

"Your father...," she began, and then changed her mind. "I don't know. Go play, skate — do something," she told them both, and made herself comfortable on the grass in the shade. Overhead, the light rail scraped by toward the nearby station.

It felt good talking about David. It made him more real. It had been a long time since she had shown an interest in a man, and longer still since she had slept with one. There was something fearful about opening herself to that kind of hurt again, but more; the energy required to get to know someone, to learn their details, nuances, intentions, actions, likes and dislikes, to become part of a whole rather than a separate, to rely on, at least in some sense, for a degree of joy — was way too much to consider. Certainly, she had desires, but they could be fleeting, and she could handle that herself. The boys' father had left her with quite a need for self-protection.

"Hi David," she said, only mouthing the words silently, smiling at the thought that he had just arrived. "I was worried about you. I thought you'd never return. I missed you. Won't you come sit and talk with me? I'd like to get to know you."

She could imagine him smiling back. In her mind, he was happy to see her, too.

"Hi, David," she said during another imagining. "Why do you stay in your car? Why don't you come and join us? I'd love to spend some time with you."

And yet again, "I'm glad you came back. Would it be possible to talk?" She liked that approach and promised herself that when he came back, she would approach him.

"David...," she said softly. And then remembered it wasn't his name.

Two weeks later, Daniel returned to the skate park. He arrived later than usual, just in case Karen had been expecting him. He pulled into his usual spot on the dirt lot, close to the fence, close to where she was, but far enough to leave quickly. He turned off the car.

Karen looked up and froze. Daniel stared at her, then smiled and quickly looked away. His heart was racing, and he could feel the hard beats of his heart. Ahead of him, Jason skated past, looked, and waved. Daniel waved back, but just enough to be noticed. He tried to relax. It felt odd.

Jason passed by again and stared at the hood of the car.

There was no dent to be seen. He rolled over to his mother and said something to her. She looked up. Jason pointed at Daniel, but Daniel could not hear what was being said. Karen stood up, nodded, brushed grass from her jeans, and patted her hair back. Daniel could see that she was about to come his way. She looked scared. He felt scared. He wasn't ready for this; he needed to stop it before it got too far.

As she started to move, he started the car. She heard it and stopped. He slipped it into reverse. She took a step toward him, and he allowed the car to roll back slightly. Karen stopped, as though facing a wild cat that was about to lunge at her sudden movement. Daniel stopped. She took another cautious step, and Daniel rolled further back. She understood and turned to walk back into the skate park.

Daniel slipped the car forward to the spot he was in, waited until she had sat back down, before turning the engine off again. He could feel her staring at him. He looked at her, smiled, and nodded. She nodded back, then turned to watch her son skate.

Daniel leaned back in his seat, his eyes scanning the park, watching the kids on deck, dancing on wheels, and defying gravity. And every few minutes, his eyes would sweep past Karen, noticing a detail here and there, the way she sat, the way her back curved, the way her hair blew forward with the slight breeze. He felt as if he had always known her and could count on her.

Here, there was no loss and no pain for him. There was no disappointment to be had, no let-downs. She could never betray him the way his wife had betrayed him. She couldn't steal his son away, never to be seen again, hiding in some unknown city under a different name. He hadn't been the one to betray her.

But here, he could still feel some joy to compensate for all that. It was good enough. It was all he could handle, at least for now. It was the best he could have or be.

ABOUT THE AUTHOR

William Gensburger is the award-winning author of Texas Dead: A Season of Death, Texas Dead: A Season of Despair, Verisium: Conversations with AI on the Meaning of Life and Death, Distant Rumors: 10 Short Stories, and more.

He is also a ghostwriter, a proficient graphic designer with decades of magazine and newspaper layout experience, and publisher of Books & Pieces Magazine (since 2017), and B&P Books, a boutique small publisher.

12

BETWIXT AND BETWEEN. A NOVELLA BY ANNIE LEMERANDE

Confusion has a large body—a big swelling stomach splayed out against its belt. It presses its weight against Bree's temples. She wasn't startled by the feeling; she had long since become an unwitting host, expecting its arrival. Still, the question came, familiar and disbelieving: Was it really going to be like this every. Single. Morning?

Bree already knew the answer was yes; life rarely offered surprises. And there lay the real bafflement: not the confusion itself, but the unshakable fact that it would feel this real, over and over, day after day.

Well, of course, until she was dead—but that thought felt a bit too dark when the sun had only just come up. It wasn't a practical notion anyway. Bree knew she would live a very long life. She thought about it rather often; it was just the plan chalked out for her. It made sense—important people were supposed to live a long time so they could get their important-people-things done. She reminded herself of this as she tossed her comforter off with self-assured urgency, though this Monday looked like it would hold all the same mundanity as the ones before it.

She smoothed the lumps in her comforter as she considered a new observation: when people die young, ordinary or not, they gain an automatic importance. It didn't seem fair how early deaths always brought a degree of shock and sadness that older ones weren't afforded. Bree pictured, just for a moment, the flowers she'd receive, the crowd that would gather just for her. But she would be more important in life than in death; she'd make certain of it. She just needed to ensure she was significant enough that when she died of old age, people would still be both thoroughly shocked and sad when she was gone.

She dreamt of her future often. Her mind would cascade down endless passages, all different and yet more remarkable than the last. But Bree understood the reality of the mind during sleep, not as a soothsayer or a place of fortune but as what it truly was: random thoughts, bubbling in irritation with the body's stillness, blurting pictures of whatever nonsense was recently on the mind. She understood this, yet still, every once in a while, quietly, she'd allow herself to imagine, somehow, perhaps, only maybe, her dreams were a window into a real place. She stayed on this thought, what a thing that would be, building a world, one that was hers and hers alone.

She would never utter such a thought out loud. Of course not, not even within her room. It was a valid concern that someone might burst from her closet with a camera at any moment, yelling, "See! I caught your confession!" This would be frustrating because the video footage wouldn't be accurate. She wasn't truly trying to float away to some made-up magical place like she was a little kid.

But it wouldn't matter. The footage would spread, and her easily convinced, weak-minded, controllable, drama-seeking peers would devour any chance to make her look naïve, an opportunity she had to ensure they would never get, even if that meant being cautious of her own thoughts.

Bree was no longer a child, and she could no longer hide behind its illusion.

Besides, she didn't have the luxury of time to think about what she truly wanted. The start of this school year had brought a new weight to her reality, and that burden could not be ignored. When she finally braced herself, pushing up from the warmth of her sheets, her responsibilities seemed to stand up with her, reminding her that time was dwindling.

These early mornings had been occurring for a month, and already, the start of her 7th-grade year had demanded a lot from Bree—a lot requiring a keen level of maturity and patience in a place that, except for her own presence, was lacking these qualities. She wouldn't say the pressure was crushing, but even she, at times, felt the strain of its relentless pace. She continued thinking on this while rolling her toothpaste tube over itself, squeezing out the last bit; while spending five minutes on her hands, wriggling under her bed to find her pants; and finally—with the swiftest motion yet—fifteen minutes later, while fastening her seatbelt before Victoria could ask her to do so.

While Victoria requesting her to buckle up may seem like a small interaction, Victoria was a human water fountain: one of those that pool sadly over their own spigots, offering little relief yet never truly shutting off. Once one comment was made, there was always another, and then the next. Little to no communication was preferable. "Victoria" was a preferable name, too. Bree preferred calling her this compared to "mother."

They were four minutes down the road, and her younger sister Emerson, in her usual performative manner, had talked nonstop so far, punctuating her monologue with loud, exasperated breaths from her car seat. Victoria tilted her head up toward the rearview mirror, glancing at her second daughter in the backseat and nodding along contentedly as she went on.

Rides to school with just Victoria and Emerson filling the air with chatter always went more smoothly than when Bree was added into the mix. This was a silent, agreed-upon understanding between the three of them, an invisible truth hovering in the air, unspoken yet obeyed. And still, it was an overly loud compromise. Bree pressed her face against the window, trying to focus instead on the gentle vibration of the road, the soft bumping echoing in her ears. She imagined herself teleporting through the glass, fast enough to swing on the branches and bounce from one oak tree to the next, leaping further and further down the valley as it rushed by outside the window.

The tires slowed as Victoria signaled to turn into the circular drive that wrapped itself around the front of the middle school. Bree didn't wait, opening her door before the car could creep any closer to the main entrance. Victoria quickly jolted on the brakes, her abrupt stop drawing an audacious laugh from the back seat. Still, Victoria's silence remained. Actually, with her deep breath, the silence seemed to broaden, as though silence itself could grow quieter. Was that possible? Apparently so.

"Have a good day," Victoria finally said once Bree was fully out of the car.

"Yep!" Bree replied, forcing an ounce of cheer into her voice.

"Bye, Sissy!"

Bree closed the door behind her, without enough time to respond, as she stepped onto the sidewalk and began to head towards the front of the school. A moment later, she heard the car pull away, heading towards the elementary school. Bree paused, turning back for just a moment. Emerson's small hand stuck out of the rolled-down window, waving more with her fingers than her full hand, until Victoria's silver car disappeared down the road. The five-minute warning bell chimed, but Bree let the sound slip away, shutting it out. She knew she had a busy day ahead. She knew she mustn't be late.

Perhaps tomorrow she would finally decide not to be late, she thought, standing on the curb for the next two minutes, watching the cars slow, stop, and drive away in a steady rhythm. She heard the screech of a bus brake releasing to her right, the final drop-off leaving. *Right*, she once again reminded herself, she really needed to make her way to the entrance.

She walked past the schoolyard, its boundaries marked by tall wooden beams that stretched out, enclosing nearly all the open land on the right side of the school's property. She couldn't see beyond the fence, but she imagined the expanse of grass stretching far and wide on the other side and immediately felt calmer. She pictured the picnic tables lining the edges, where they were allowed to eat lunch when it was warm enough, and the adjacent playground, which was mostly lame unless you were a sixth grader— except, of course, for the monkey bars. Before P.E., while the rest of her class ambled outside at their usual slow pace, she'd sprint to those large metal bars, hoisting herself to the top of them to gaze down at the schoolyard underneath her.

She reached out, dragging her fingers along the smooth wood, careful not to step off the path onto the grass. The schoolyard sat on a hill, and after every rain, water pooled stubbornly at the bottom of the fence, never quite freeing the beams from the soggy grass and muddy patches. But even if a hurricane swept the entire schoolyard into a muddy swamp, Bree would still come back, spotting the top of her monkey bars above the water and leaping to their safety. The schoolyard was the only redeeming quality of this place, the only reason Bree kept returning. Honestly, the only reason most students did. Without that lot of land, she figured, the school would have to close its doors due to zero enrollment.

The school's enrollment numbers were already low enough. It was a small Catholic school, one that even most parents wouldn't force their children to attend. Bree imagined most of the teachers secretly wished to hit the lot of them, if only the students didn't all have phones ready to record such entertainment. She and her peers who were stuck here had practically grown up together, trapped first at the Catholic elementary school and now confined within these walls, too. New students almost never arrive at the middle school. Last year, Bree would have said, literally, no new students entered this place. Unfortunately, she was wrong about that. This rare moment of being wrong occurred a month ago, when Alice walked into Bree's English class for the first time.

She took a deep breath, trying to shove thoughts of Alice aside as she reached the entrance. Bree had already felt worked up, *like*, three times today, and she hadn't even made it through the school doors yet!

She rang the buzzer; at three minutes past the start of school, the door was now locked. Mary, from behind her small desk, peered down over her spectacles, looking out through the glass doors. Bree didn't like being looked at in this manner (it made her feel short, and she really was rather tall), but she didn't protest—no time. Instead, she smiled at Mary as apologetically as she could manage, and the woman obliged. Once the penitentiary doors were unlocked, Bree escorted herself to her first class.

Her classroom's door had not been left open for her, but no matter. She swung it open as far as it would go, the impact snapping pleasantly against the doorstop. Miss Tulip turned abruptly, and the entire class followed suit—well, almost. Dead center in the front row, Alice kept her eyes fixed on the book splayed open in front of her, as if it were more captivating than Bree. *Most certainly it couldn't have been.*

But no matter, Bree didn't look at her either! Instead, she met Miss Tulip's gaze just as the teacher addressed her. "Nice of you to join us, Bree."

Bree gave a two-finger salute in response and headed for her seat in the back of the English classroom.

ONCE BREE REACHED HER DESK, Miss Tulip continued with her plodding monologue, a book open in her hands, the students silently reading along with their own textbooks. Bree quickly rummaged through her backpack, pulling out her copy of *A Guide to Writing Personal Essays*. In an inconvenient, uncontrollable sense, she felt a tightness in her chest as she rapidly flipped through the pages, none of them looking familiar. Miss Tulip's mouth seemed to be increasing in speed, Bree not able to quite make sense of her words. She leaned toward Jeremy, who was sitting next to her, trying to make out the small letters at the bottom of his page.

"It's page 46," he finally whispered. Bree couldn't help hearing an edge of something sharp in his voice.

Bree slouched back in her chair. Jeremy was her dearest friend, but lately, during English class, their friendship no longer seemed to hold his attention. He was always scanning his textbook, diligently following along with Miss Tulip's words. Before this year, Bree hadn't even known he could read. She took her focus away from him, glancing towards the clock.

She did understand that this kept happening, her being late, but within these walls, where they so desperately wanted her and her classmates to stand in neat little lines like robots, it felt important that she show her individuality. She was capable of this because she didn't possess fear the way her classmates did. That was what made them so very obedient. Bree didn't fault them for this. Fear was a debilitating thing. At least, this is what she would assume, not knowing the feeling herself.

At least she didn't try to stand out in the embarrassing ways some of her classmates did. Drew and Brady, the grade's main rebellious culprits, came to mind. Their rebellions took shape through spitballs fired from straws, chairs pulled out from beneath unsuspecting students, and crude messages scrawled on the dry-erase board. It was all rather comical to Bree, though not in the way they intended. It was laughable because of how juvenile it all was.

Childishness never accomplished anything. Bree knew why this was, but it was something she did not like to think about too often, a secret she kept buried deep down in her gut. If one of her teachers, or worse, her parents, found out that she had figured it out, and that she saw the world a little too clearly, they might expect even more from her than they already did. She was already stretched far too thin. Still, if she ever caught herself craving a similar shape of rebellion, one that made her look like a child, she reminded herself of that secret, making sure to maintain her behavior in an appropriate fashion.

"Bree, what about you?"

Bree snapped her head back to Miss Tulip's voice, retreating from the window her thoughts had wandered to.

"What? Sorry," she replied, trying to regain focus.

Miss Tulip repeated herself. "What has been the largest difficulty in writing the personal essay about responsibility for you?"

The most difficult part, Bree wanted to say, wasn't the writing itself but having to listen to her classmates ramble on about what they deemed a *tough* responsibility, as if taking care of a goldfish amounted to any real burden.

Bree chewed on her cheek for a moment, then replied with quick, formidable words. "I have found it rather easy!"

Miss Tulip seemed disappointed by her answer. This was not Bree's fault, but the teacher's. Perhaps the only one who fit less in this classroom than Alice was Miss Tulip. It was Bree's first year having her as a teacher, but her reputation was as strikingly accurate as her glitter-dusted dry-erase board. While most of the classrooms were occupied with hushed whispers and controlling stares, Miss Tulip's class was always LOUD.

If a student had a rebuttal for the teacher, she welcomed it! If a student wanted to share a random, irrelevant, not-exciting-at-all story, she applauded! If the simplest assignment elicited ten questions for clarification from the class, she asked for an eleventh! Normally, this would have just been inconvenient to Bree, but within this class, it was a major problem because Alice talked more than anyone else Bree had ever met.

After Bree's accurate, but for some reason insufficient response, Alice's hand shot into the air with such ferocity that Bree thought it might pop out of the socket. Her fingers wiggled frantically, as if Miss Tulip, standing just a few feet away, couldn't see her.

The teacher turned away from Bree, letting out an audible sigh as she nodded toward Alice.

"For me, the most difficult part of writing about responsibility has been…" Alice began.

Bree tried, as she did most mornings, to distract herself from Alice's voice, thinking about something else instead. Today, she thought about Miss Tulip. She wondered if that had been her name from birth, or if it was a name she had chosen for herself, something she decided suited her better than whatever one had come before. If it had been a choice, Bree felt sad that she wanted something so delicate to encapsulate herself. Bree would make sure her own name meant more than that.

Bree thought on this for a moment, but she kept getting inconveniently distracted by Alice's voice. It was high-pitched and squeaky, like a little mouse. Alice threw the words out of her mouth quickly, as if any moment the oxygen in the room might be stolen from her. She also didn't put her hand down while she talked, as if she thought that when she finally lowered it, the class would forget she was talking. Which, to be fair, Bree believed they might.

Ruby, sitting right in front of Bree, turned back towards her, smacking her gum with aggressive boredom and rolling her eyes as Alice's seemingly 100-word run-on sentence continued to stream out of her mouth.

Bree mouthed Alice's words, mimicking her. "The challenge has been fun." Though she aimed the words at Ruby, she glanced towards Jeremy, hoping to make him laugh.

But Jeremy just scratched his neck, tucking his hands into his green sweatshirt, not giving any inclination that he had heard Bree. Ruby giggled at Bree's impression, running her fingers through a smooth strand of her brunette hair. The noise prompted Miss Tulip to look towards the back of the class, and Jeremy cleared his throat with a warning, causing Ruby to quickly return her focus to the front of the room.

"That's a great point, Alice," the teacher finally said. Alice would have probably kept talking if not cut off. Miss Tulip headed towards the board. "It can best be explained like this," she said, picking up a marker.

The other students followed the teacher's hand up to the board, but Bree stayed fixated on the back of Alice's head, which was bobbing along excessively while the teacher began to write. The problem wasn't just her voice. Alice's entire demeanor was rather mouse-like. It wasn't as much what she wore but how it fit her. Today, she had a dress with large, bulky sleeves that slithered down her arms when she raised them (so, like, every five minutes!). Her dress screamed dishtowel. Bree imagined it smelled, though she had never gotten close enough to confirm this suspicion. Alice's thrown-together appearance mirrored the large, dirty-blonde ringlets spiraling out from every inch of her head in disarray. Bree focused on one of the puffy ringlets, thinking about it springing off Alice's head.

"Does anyone have any questions before we pick our reader of the day?" asked Miss Tulip.

Bree immediately felt flushed at the thought of Alice having another question, so, for the sake of the class, she made a sacrifice. She called Miss Tulips' name, raising her hand more as a half-hearted wave than a formal request to speak, and began talking before being called on. "I need help back here!" It was a proclamation.

Alice turned quickly, her fingers pointing up from her desk as if she was about to speak, but when she made eye contact with Bree, she quickly turned back around.

Bree smirked at her triumph, but then remembered that she needed to think of a question, quickly scanning her book.

"Yes, Bree?" Miss Tulip approached her desk.

"Yep . . . just one moment . . .." she smacked her pointer finger down on a random sentence. "Just wanted you to tell me what this word means!" she said, pointing to the longest word she could find on the page.

The teacher looked down at the page, back up towards Bree, then down again. She read the word Bree's finger sat underneath. "Introspection," she emphasized, and then continued reading the sentence: "The examination or observation of one's own mental and emotional process-es..." She stopped abruptly, looking back up towards her student unamused, "Does that clear it up for you?"

"Yep," Bree said with a forced smile.

Miss Tulip cleared her throat and turned back towards the front of the classroom.

A gentle chortle left Jeremy's throat as the teacher walked away, prompting a shove in his shoulder from Bree. But Bree had accomplished what she needed. Next, Miss Tulip said it was time for someone to read out loud, and there was no more time for another of Alice's questions.

Bree knew that another part of Miss Tulips' *different* classroom philosophy was that she didn't feel obliged to force anyone to read against their will, which prompted all the students to freeze their hands to their seats like little icicles when it was time to volunteer to read their most recent writing assignment. Well, all but one.

Miss Tulip scanned the room as if Alice's raised hand were invisible. Perhaps even the teacher was bored of her voice, her being the classroom's reader the last two days. Bree felt a pang, her shoulders tensing slightly. As much as she wanted to save the class from another of Alice's incessant readings, this was a sacrifice even she couldn't make.

"I really don't mind reading again!" Alice called out, ignoring the fact that she herself was getting ignored.

The teacher waited another moment, as if expecting a hand to suddenly appear in the air, though she must have known it wouldn't. Her eyes shifted to the back row, making Bree's breath catch. Wait—was she looking at her? A pang tightened in Bree's chest at the thought that Miss Tulip might have lost her senses and was actually considering calling on her.

But then, just as quickly, her gaze drifted again. "That's fine, Alice," she said, turning towards her.

Bree's breath settled again, but a taste of bile lingered in the back of her throat as she watched Alice spring up from her desk, skipping eagerly toward the front of the classroom. Bree checked the clock, trying to hold on until P.E., which, while it seemed to be ticking closer with the second hand, simultaneously seemed to be getting increasingly further away as Alice began to read. Her voice was rapid as she read from a loose-leaf piece of paper, which seemed to be covered in the smallest print imaginable.

Ruby yawned dramatically, slumping onto her forearms.

Bree's focus flicked to the side of the classroom. Jeremy wasn't paying attention either, which didn't surprise her. Actually, though, Jeremy wasn't just staring off into nowhere like most of the other students. He was intently focused on his lap, where his hands were hidden under the table.

Bree leaned back slightly to see what he was looking at. He was holding a single piece of loose-leaf paper. It wasn't covered in writing; from her angle, it looked like just a few scattered words running down the length of the page, all placed in choppy, little sections. Jeremy's eyes scanned over them repeatedly, as if each time he read a word, he immediately forgot it.

If there was anyone who was likely to find reading out loud more of a nuisance than she did, she assumed it was Jeremy… *Oh no!* A terrifying thought entered her head.

Did the format look so strange because they were jokes? Had he really decided to stoop to the level of classroom pranks like Drew and Brady?! Jeremy truly held more substance than childish pranks; she certainly wished he'd act like it.

Bree had to put a stop to this before he embarrassed himself—and her, too.

"What did you want to read?" Bree whispered toward him.

Jeremy looked up at her sharply, clearly not realizing she had been watching him. His eyes widened for just a second, then he let out a quiet laugh and shook his head.

"Oh. Nah! It's nothing," he said, crumpling the paper slightly as he folded it in half and slid it into his pocket, straightening his posture slightly.

Bree thought about how she should proceed. Should she accept that he had gone momentarily insane, or call him out on the behavior so it wouldn't happen again? But just as she was thinking it over, the bell rang, and Jeremy immediately stood up, shoving his textbook into his backpack in one fluid motion.

All the other students began to grab their backpacks too, well, except for Alice. As if the bell had nothing to do with her, she kept reading. Bree was unsure if she had paused for air once, and at this rate, her face might swell up any moment from the lack of oxygen.

Bree glanced toward Miss Tulip, who was still nodding along contentedly as Alice sped up her words to an almost inaudible level.

"And that's why getting good grades is an important responsibility! The end!" she finally wheezed out.

She looked around, as if waiting for applause of some sort, but all the students were already halfway into the hallway. Bree was the second one out, staying close to Jeremy's heels.

AN HOUR AND A HALF LATER, Bree was in position out in the schoolyard. She gripped the metal of the monkey bars beneath her arms, her knees tucked under her like a hawk. She watched as the rest of her class poured out through the double doors into the sunlight, their khakis traded for gym shorts, their polos swapped for tees. The most important hour of the day was finally beginning, even if the school administration did not grasp the significance of this hour, as evidenced by their choice of P.E. teacher, Mrs. Stitchley, standing, well, as best she could, off to the side of the doors.

The only part of Mrs. Stitchley more arched than her old back was her furrowed eyebrows. The teacher would have loved to hit the lot of them, Bree was sure of it. She probably would have, too, if the physical exertion hadn't almost certainly left her brittle spine snapping in half. Instead, Mrs. Stitchley clung to her usual scowl as she slowly marked down names on her clipboard.

In front of Bree, the other students bolted in different directions, savoring their freedom before Mrs. Stitchley's raspy voice signaled the start of class. One group huddled on the sidewalk, speaking in the loudest hushed voices they could muster. At one of the picnic tables, a group of girls sat, quickly braiding one another's hair, pulling it back in preparation for P.E., as if a few stray flyaways were the reason they were slow runners.

Bree set her eyes on her friends. They didn't wait at the picnic tables but stepped proudly onto the large grass field. Ruby, now picking at her cuticles, had pulled her hair back, making sure to carefully place a few curls down the sides of her face. Jeremy scuffed at the grass impatiently. He had changed into a light blue shirt. Bree took note that blue was certainly his color, although she had said the same thing about green the previous week.

Drew and Brady barreled onto the field, tugging at each other's T-shirts with over-aggressive enthusiasm as they joined Jeremy and Ruby at the center of the field. Bree sighed in disappointment. Drew and Brady's behavior was just so very… fourth grade. She didn't exactly enjoy being around them. But no matter—they were two of her closest friends. More importantly, they were the only two in the entire grade taller than her, which, in her mind, made them impressive enough to be worth keeping around.

Suddenly, another group of students stepped onto the field, keeping their distance from her friends. They lingered near the edge of the fence, edging dangerously close to the top of the hill that sloped down toward the hazardous mud pools. Imagine it—running, slipping, drenching yourself in the most unpleasant brown imaginable. Just the thought made Bree's arm tremble beneath her. While the stench of the mud could eventually be scrubbed, the humiliation would linger, altering a person irreparably.

Speaking of humiliating, Alice had finally made her way outside. Bree figured she might as well not have changed out of her classroom attire; the T-shirt she had on was far too long, blending into her equally long shorts, which hung past her knees, resembling a dress of their own. Alice's attempt at sporty clothing expressed to Bree how unprepared she was for physical activity of any kind. Unlike Alice, Bree's outfit was perfectly balanced, a plain shirt without any silly designs, like so many of her classmates wore, and a nice pair of shorts that weren't too long to restrict her movements.

Alice didn't step onto the field or wait at one of the picnic tables. Instead, she hovered by the edge of the sidewalk, scuffing at the grass with her shoe, as if stepping on it before the teacher would cause the strange green substance to eat her alive. Bree watched as she raised her hand from the sidewalk, waving enthusiastically toward the field. Bree wasn't sure who the gesture was meant for, while a few students glanced her way, no one as much as smiled back. Just as Bree began to wonder if Alice's hand might be stuck midair, a student on the field finally acknowledged her, hesitantly lifting his hand and giving it two half-hearted swipes before quickly letting it drop again. No one else seemed to notice, but Bree certainly did. She narrowed her eyes at Alice, who lowered her hand triumphantly, beaming as if the entire student body had just acknowledged her.

Bree closed her eyes and took a deep breath, trying to calm herself as she wondered whether she had ever seen a similar exchange before. She didn't think so; her observational skills would have caught it. But after what she had just witnessed, she couldn't be too sure of anything, or anyone, in that moment. Clearly, her entrance was needed before more people started exhibiting bizarre behavior. Twisting her body, she swung off the side of the monkey bars, keeping her eyes locked on Jeremy, the culprit behind the returned wave.

Bree was still crossing the field when Ruby's high-pitched voice cut through the air.

"Can you, like… stop that?" she pleaded, motioning for Drew to remove Brady's face from where it was shoved firmly under his armpit.

Drew didn't release him. "Are you going to make me?" he replied, stifling a laugh, which promptly earned him an uppercut to the ribs from Brady's free fist.

Ruby opened her mouth to respond, but as quickly as her attention was gained, it was stolen, her head snapping past Drew. "Ty!" she squealed.

Bree had made her way to her group, earning only a

quick nod from Jeremy and no acknowledgment at all from the other three. Brady's face remained lodged at Drew's side, while Drew's was now plastered with disappointment as Ruby's attention shifted away from him. Ruby scurried past the group, heading straight for Tyler who was striding onto the field with his shoulders pulled back so far Bree thought they might dislocate.

If Bree had to think subjectively, Tyler was the only one faster than her in their grade, but he still hadn't earned a spot in her group. He mostly hung out with 8th graders, which was rather desperate. The mere thought of hanging out with a 6th grader was enough to make Bree's spine shiver. However, Ruby hadn't thought this through as thoroughly as Bree had, which was quite evident as the space between her and Tyler shrank with every one of his broad strides.

Mrs. Stitchley finally wobbled onto the field with the supplies for kickball, well, at least some of them, five bases stacked in her arms. The rubber ball for the game was clutched against Alice's chest as she followed in tow behind the teacher.

Before it got too cold and they were forced to move P.E. indoors, they almost exclusively played kickball. Bree speculated it might be the only game Mrs. Stitchley knew existed. Bree was just making an observation, not complaining. She very much liked the game. The teacher threw down the makeshift bases, and three students eagerly shuffled over to set them out in their diamond formation.

"Teams!" the teacher croaked. That was all she said, as if the single word held all the instruction they could possibly need. Which, in her defense, it really did. Tyler and Drew were the team leaders. This wasn't discussed or debated. It was just an obvious truth.

"Jeremy," Drew called his first teammate. While he'd pick Brady next, he had to pick Jeremy first, before Tyler's team got a chance. It wasn't personal—just smart business.

A few of the other boys had been called, then Bree was called to Drew's team. She was always the first girl to be picked, way ahead of the rest.

"Ruby," Tyler said next.

Bree snapped her head in his direction. *Seriously?* Ruby waddled the bases like a penguin! If Tyler was going to start picking players based on something other than athletic ability, maybe he shouldn't be team captain at all, Bree thought, narrowing her eyes at him.

Once all the desirable players had been picked, Tyler and Brady had been reluctantly forced to choose from the remaining students. The students left were the ones who stared blankly into space during the game, dragged their feet with no interest in playing, or worse, those whose heads might have wanted to participate but whose bodies clearly disagreed, moving with the grace of someone who had never attempted an athletic activity in their life. With her small physique, irritable behavior in class, and new-student status, Alice had secured the role of last pick for the past month.

Worse than all of that, Bree was convinced Alice carried bad luck around with her. Every time Bree's team had lost, she was pretty sure Alice had been on it. Even when they had relegated her to the furthest spot in the outfield, where the ball never landed, and the very back of the lineup, where she never got a chance to kick before the team struck out, somehow Alice's unlucky nature still seemed to infect the rest of the team. Fortunately, when it was Drew's final turn to pick, there were still two players left, and Alice trotted over to Tyler's team by default for the day when Drew did not pick her.

The gameplay began, and Bree's team was up to kick first. She was seventh in the lineup, placed ahead of the other girls. She shook out her hands, preparing for her turn. When it came, she executed the kick perfectly. While the ball didn't lift into the air, it rolled sharply to the left, picking up speed as it cascaded down the hill toward the wooden fence, a strategic move that gave her enough time to sprint all the way to second base. By the time the ball was returned to the pitcher's mound, she was firmly planted on the base, choosing to hold her position rather than risk being struck out on her way to third.

Bree caught her breath, waiting for her next teammate to kick. For a brief moment, she shifted her focus to the outfield. In one of the furthest corners stood Alice. Her arms were stretched above her head, eyes fixed on home base, as if the ball, which hadn't been kicked that far once since the start of seventh grade, might suddenly head her way. Perhaps persistence could be admirable in some cases, but here? Bree was almost certain the girl might be just a little bit unhinged.

WHEN THE LAST bell of the school day rang, Bree was one of the first outside. She glanced back at her classmates, tripping over their backpack straps as they scrambled toward freedom. She walked quickly past the students gathered at the curb, peering around the corner for their rides. Bree didn't have time to wait. She headed toward the spot where she had gotten out of the car that morning, passing the wooden fence quickly, not because she was eager to get home, but because she liked the view from the top of the sidewalk.

Once she reached her destination, Bree turned her focus back toward the school's entrance. Jeremy was standing there, not looking for his mother's blue car with the small dent in the side, but up at the sky. He looked at it like it was more to him than the dull far, faraway yellow circle it was to her, which was probably true. Things always seemed brighter to him; she had taken note of this. Sometimes it made her frown, knowing that one day all that brightness would erupt across his peaceful face. But sometimes, for a reason she couldn't quite explain, it made her stomach settle in a way it rarely did.

She shifted her head toward the road. Victoria, who always seemed unhurried picking up Emerson, was nowhere in sight, so Bree turned back towards him. Jeremy's head was now tilted to the right. She was too far away to make out exactly what she was seeing, but his jaw moved slightly, working up and down in conversation—though Bree didn't see anyone near him.

Wait... what was...?! She took a step closer, squinting.

Jeremy shifted his stance, and that was when Bree saw it. The fabric of her dress, her small figure hidden behind his stature. She folded her hand against her heart, her breath leaving her at the sight of such a betrayal.

Alice!

Bree's hands balled into fists, her mind churning frantically. What could he possibly have been talking to her about? Never once had she seen such a thing! And now there had been two interactions today, surely this just could not be...

Jolted from such a horrific image, Bree turned reflexively at the sound of her name being shouted. Drew leaned off the seat of his bike, an inch from her ear.

"Seriously, Drew!" she snapped, shoving him in the shoulder. For arguably the loudest member of her grade, Drew could sneak up on someone when he wanted to.

He laughed, settling onto his bike's seat. "Staring at Jeremy, are we?" he asked in his usual daunting tone.

Bree gathered her composure quickly. She wouldn't give him the satisfaction of getting a rise out of her.

"Just looking at the only reason we didn't lose kickball again today, Cap," she said coolly. She didn't use the title as praise, but as a reminder. If he was no longer deserving to hold onto it, someone else would be ready to take his place.

They held eye contact for a moment, her smirk increasing as his dulled.

"Whatever," he finally muttered, setting his right foot on the pedal and bolting away a second later, as if someone were timing his speed.

Right on cue, *late*, she saw Victoria's car approaching from the opposite direction. As the car neared, she noticed Emerson's crazed wave—her fingers moving sporadically like little spiders, sticking themselves out of the window.

Bree glanced back towards Drew, making sure he had biked considerably down the road. Then, subtly, she shifted her gaze once again toward the school, but as if it had all been a dream, or a nightmare, Jeremy was on the curb by himself once again. He waved as the little blue car pulled up in front of him. Bree kept her eyes there until he was fully inside the car, gone in a fleeting moment.

FIFTEEN MINUTES into Miss Tulip's class the next morning, Bree's chin slid down her palm, only for her to prop it back up again with an audible sigh. She was certain her distress was radiating off her, tilting her head towards Jeremy to check, but he must not have noticed. His focus was isolated on his English textbook once again, which was becoming an increasing problem. It made Bree look down at her own copy with disgust, the black ink taunting her with its overbearing word count.

Back and forth her thoughts bounced as she revisited her sentiments from yesterday. Had such interactions between Alice and Jeremy happened before?! She tried to convince herself of the opposite. Maybe the events from yesterday were just so forgettable to Jeremy that he did not even think to mention it to Bree. But she knew how Jeremy so often sat with every moment of life as if each one was worth the memory. Would this be any different?

The longer Bree stared at the back of Alice's head, with those fluffy curls tied into a nest, the more flushed her skin felt. Then, in painful, predictable slow motion, the girl's spindly arm shot into the air to answer a question. As she began to speak, the entire room felt like it might combust.

Bree tried to squeeze herself down into a mental tunnel, blocking out Alice's voice. If Bree had been concerned about her learning, now would have been the time to panic. The girl spent so much time asking questions that there was barely any room for Miss Tulip to progress in a lesson. It was becoming increasingly obvious to Bree that Alice knew nothing about the proper way to be a student, an appropriate level of talking to a teacher, and certainly nothing about an appropriate level of talking to Jeremy. Which was zero!

Bree could not help but be drawn back into the classroom chatter as Miss Tulip's voice grew in volume. "Would anyone like to share their writing … besides Alice?"

Even Miss Tulip, it seemed, had grown tired of hearing Alice's voice. And while Bree felt the same, she slouched low in her chair, eyes glued to the floor. After the day she had yesterday, standing in front of the class and reading aloud felt like the one thing that could actually make the start of this day worse.

A quick thumbing, sounding like a strangled rabbit, caught her attention to the left of the room, where Jeremy's foot bounced rapidly against the floor. The movement rippled up his body. Bree could see his arms, firmly placed on something hidden beneath his desk.

She gently pushed her chair back to get a better view of whatever had possessed him. Jeremy's fingers fidgeted against the lines of a small piece of loose-leaf paper. It looked to Bree like the same paper from the day before, but unlike then, it was now folded in half, as if he were trying to avoid looking at the words.

Bree retracted her earlier sentiment. Actually, this was

the one thing that could possibly make the start of this day even worse. The only attribute she hated more than childishness was fear, and somehow Jeremy had become the kind of person who seemed to overwhelmingly possess both. Bree's skin felt flushed as she thought about the kind of person Jeremy was *choosing* to be. She knew it was a choice because she also knew the seriousness and substance he could project into the world if he only tried. Bree believed he was holding that version of himself hostage in his own mind. She could tell by the way he sat with his thoughts, as if each one was worth rehashing. But how much longer could she wait for him to snap out of his childish ways? She had grown tired of his newfound secrets, his newfound inability to apparently talk in this class, but be able to exhaust plenty of communication with Alice outside of it!

The admiration she had felt yesterday, when Jeremy chose not to share whatever jokes he had written, had been completely replaced by disdain for his inability to just make up his mind. The thoughts overflowed within her. That was it! If he wanted to embarrass himself, so be it! If he couldn't be brave, she would have to take matters into her own hands again!

"Jeremy would like to read his!" The words exploded from her rapidly as her head felt like it was about to burst.

Jeremy snapped his head to her quickly, looking at her with… what was that, disbelief?

"What?" she said loudly. "You're already ready!" She leaned over her desk. "He's got it right here!" she told the class.

As she reached for his arm, he pulled away quickly, standing up from his seat almost on impulse.

The class, now turned toward him, shifted its gaze to the paper visible in his hand.

"Wait, you, like, know how to write?" Ruby asked loudly.

A burst of laughter erupted from the classroom before they were hushed by Miss Tulip.

Jeremy ignored Ruby's comment, keeping his focus on Bree. His eyebrows furrowed at her for a moment as he crinkled his paper and shoved it into his pocket, but then he quickly regained his composure, turning towards the teacher with a neutral expression.

"Can I go to the restroom, Miss Tulip?" he asked.

The teacher's approval came out as a quick wheeze, but even if she had said no, Jeremy was already halfway to the door.

Well... that was an overreaction. Bree folded her arms and leaned back, sinking into the uncomfortable silence that had settled over the classroom. Outbursts like that were an incessant waste of time, never accomplishing anything. Bree knew why, but she had already visited that secret truth yesterday and didn't want to dwell on it again today. She had to be cautious, just in case an adult stared at her for too long and began to see the thoughts she kept right at the edge of her mind. If they saw, then they would know that she knew that they knew that she knew that such dramatic behavior only proved what the adults already thought of them. *Them,* the category Bree belonged to against her will: adolescence.

Bree was still thinking about Jeremy's melodramatics when her head nearly exploded at the sound of her name.

"I think, since she said it was so easy, that Bree could read hers."

The statement wasn't directed at Bree but at the teacher, the voice's squeaky little occupant not even bothering to turn around when she called Bree out.

Miss Tulip looked from the front row to the third row, and for the first time, perhaps ever, Bree thought she saw real irritation cross her teacher's face.

"Alice and Bree," she gulped loudly, "let's be reminded that nobody in this class volunteers others." Bree took note of the fake smile that stretched too wide across the teacher's face, as if it might slice into her ears.

"It is their choice!" The words protruded from Miss Tulip's forced expression. The room felt tight, as if the walls were made of latex, and someone had finally released the pressure.

That day in class, nobody ended up sharing their reading. For the rest of class, the silence held. Students pretended to read their textbooks while Miss Tulip stared at a stack of papers behind her desk. No voice rose above the gentle sound of the teacher's chair swaying back and forth and the occasional pop of Ruby's gum, and when the bell rang ten minutes later, Jeremy still hadn't returned.

Bree slung her backpack over her right shoulder, then reached for Jeremy's, pulling it up and holding it against her chest as the chatter finally rose when all the students began to escape towards the hallway.

Well, almost all of them.

Once at the door, Bree turned back before leaving. There was Alice, with a face as pink as a rat, hovering by the corner of Miss Tulip's desk. She appeared to be in the middle of some apologetic tangent, clearly groveling to stay on the teacher's good side. Not that Bree believed anyone could associate the word *good* with Alice in the first place, but still, the sniveling was unbearable. It was really time someone sewed that girl's lips shut, Bree thought, smacking the door against its hinges as she left.

IF THE MONKEY bars broke under the pressure of Bree's grip, it would not have been a surprise. She scanned the crowd quickly at the start of P.E., more out of duty than care, only wanting to focus her vision on one person. There was Alice, standing on the grass, waiting for Mrs. Stitchley, probably trying to slither her way toward more praise. Again.

The teacher made her way down the sidewalk, and with Alice stepped onto the field together. Her old neck wrinkled as she threw her head back with a smile at something Alice must have said.

Bree twitched her jaw. It was time for this game of kickball to get started, and time to bring Alice's games to an end. Perhaps Bree had been playing this all wrong. Ostracizing Alice to the outfield and the end of the kicking lineup was clearly not giving her the hint about where she belonged. Maybe instead, Alice needed to be thrown into the center of the game. Perhaps then, when she inevitably embarrassed herself in front of everyone, she would realize that nobody cares how many questions she gets right in class, and that she's not as superior as she clearly thinks she is!

The next five minutes were familiar. After sliding through the metal rings of the monkey bars and heading toward the field, Mrs. Stitchley called for the students to make teams. Bree was picked for Drew's team, selected before any of the other girls, and, unlike yesterday, picked significantly earlier than the other girls like she was used to. Actually, Tyler didn't call Ruby to his team at all. She scowled at him until Drew eventually picked her instead.

Trouble in Paradise, apparently.

After being picked, Bree walked towards Drew, her next movements not holding their usual routine. A sharp current buzzed down her fingertips. She stepped right next to Drew's side, cupping her palm as she whispered into his ear. Drew raised a quizzical eyebrow, but she knew he would oblige with what she had said. He wasn't the type to turn down a little unexpected excitement.

There were only two players left to be picked.

"Alice," Drew called.

Her eyes darted toward him, scanning his face hesitantly, as if wondering whether he meant a different Alice. The field fell silent, even the smacking of Ruby's gum stopping as her jaw hung open. Since the start of school, this was the first game where Alice hadn't been shuffled onto a team by default. It was the first game for which she had been picked.

Alice began to walk cautiously toward them, her team, as Bree scanned the expressions of the other students, most of them staring at Drew in disbelief. Her gaze stopped on Jeremy. His focus was not on Drew but fixed on Alice, an unreadable expression strewn across his face. Bree tasted bile in the back of her throat, but she pushed it down quickly and turned her attention back toward Drew.

The two teams moved to their starting positions, Tyler's team spreading out while Drew's lined up behind home base to kick. Bree stayed close to Drew, speaking in a hushed voice. He nodded quickly and eagerly to every word.

As the students shuffled into their usual spots, Drew called out to the player at the end of the line. The entire lineup turned to stare when he asked Alice to move up to the spot behind Bree. Slowly, she obliged, moving up the line as whispers of disapproval rose just loud enough for her to hear.

Bree and Alice didn't speak once she took her new spot, Alice keeping her gaze fixed on the pitcher's mound. But Bree couldn't help but notice that Alice's face had softened past its usual stern lines, a foreign shape beginning to take hold of her mouth, not quite a smile, but something close to it.

Both Brady and Bree had struck out. Of course, Bree striking out was her choice. Today, she knew it was more important to focus on the future, to choose the distant reward over the immediate one. Now, only Drew was on base, and Alice was up next, with one strike left. When Alice walked toward home plate, the usual furrow of her brow resumed its place on her face. Bree was unsure if Alice would even make it all the way to the plate. With her tentative steps, her body seemed like it might cocoon and solidify at any second.

Tyler rolled his neck from the makeshift pitcher's

mound as he waited, the ball, twice the size of Alice's head, firmly clenched in his grip. Finally, Alice stepped up to the base. Bree was unsure if Alice was breathing; her entire body looked rigid. Even from where she stood, Bree could see Tyler's eyes tighten with amusement. He rolled his shoulder, swinging the ball behind him with intensity.

Then, the moment the ball left his hand, something shifted, not just in Alice's face, but in her entire posture. With a gentle bend of her knees, she placed her left foot in front of her right. The sight felt strange to Bree, as if it weren't correctly fixed to reality.

Next, the ball was an inch from Alice. She bent her right leg behind her, twisted her foot outward, and then snapped it forward with such speed that the rubber ball seemed to morph against her ankle for a split second before it catapulted away from her. Nearly as fast as the ball soared over the opposing team's heads, Alice bolted toward first base, the pounding of her feet the only sound as her class-mates fell deathly silent in shock.

Drew didn't move for a moment, but then, as if he suddenly remembered he was still in the game, he began running toward the next base. Bree stared at him as he finally took off, but realized she might be the only one looking in his direction. All around her, voices were rising. Members of her team at the back of the lineup were clap-ping their hands in a frenzy. They were all looking at Alice, and they didn't laugh at her like Bree had expected; they were cheering for her. When Bree finally looked back at Alice, she would have stopped herself from being surprised if only the reaction hadn't been so involuntary.

Alice's steps replaced one another faster than seemed

possible. Bree turned her gaze to the outfield, where the opposing team was stumbling over themselves in a panic to get the ball, Tyler leading the pack, but Alice had already darted past second base. She stretched her arms as she ran, fingers spread wide, like Alice thought she could catch the wind itself. Bree couldn't place the reason why, but the image looked familiar to her. But she was quickly severed from the feeling, jolted back to the present moment when the chants for Alice grew louder, urging her to run faster. Tyler had gotten hold of the ball.

In the midst of the noise, Drew had made it to home plate, his arms outstretched like a hawk in triumph as he sprinted over the base. But the crowd was still focused on Alice, who had just made it past third. Tyler was running back toward the pitcher's mound, aiming and launching the ball toward home.

Alice's focus didn't waver. She dove toward the plate, her small body slicing through the air horizontally before landing in the grass and slapping her hand against the base as the ball bounced off her back.

"Safe!" one of her teammates yelled. Alice brought herself up to her knees, heaving for breath.

"What! So not safe!" Tyler yelled as he jogged toward them.

"Agreed!" Drew chimed in, even though it had been his own team that had scored the run.

No matter how unfortunate or unbelievable, Bree knew Alice had been safe before the ball hit her. While Bree wasn't a cheater, she also didn't feel the need to actively undermine her own plan. So, she chose to stay silent, hoping the others would agree with the team captains.

Even if some had cheered for Alice, Bree knew no one would directly stand up to Drew or Tyler.

"Mrs. Stitchley, Tyler's cheating!" Ruby yelled up towards the closest picnic table, where the teacher sat.

Well, anyone besides Ruby, apparently.

Mrs. Stitchley, who was technically the "referee," although she had never actually been called on to assume that duty, jolted her attention up from her newspaper. She tried to find where the voice had come from, but Ruby's attention was locked on Tyler. They stared at each other with such intensity that Bree honestly felt a little uncomfortable and turned to look at the teacher instead.

Mrs. Stitchley glanced around in confusion, as if she had entirely forgotten the students were even there. She blinked a few times, then finally settled her eyes on Alice, who was still kneeling on home base.

After a long beat of silence, Ruby turned back toward the teacher.

"Our entire team saw that Alice was safe, and Tyler is trying to say she wasn't."

"Yeah!" some of the teammates finally got the courage to speak up.

Drew said nothing. Tyler was still looking at Ruby, stunned.

Mrs. Stitchley stared at Alice for a moment longer. Bree saw a brief smile cross the woman's lips.

"Safe!" she proclaimed loudly, then looked back down at her newspaper without another word.

The students were silent for a minute, but no one offered a rebuttal. Alice stood up slowly, then she hoisted her fists into the air, yelling in triumph. A beat later, some of her teammates followed the motion. It seemed to Bree that they felt they had found a new puppeteer.

The wind brushed by coolly, but the back of Bree's neck was seething hot, confused by how her plan had backfired so badly. With the taste of irritation lingering in her mouth, she peeled her focus away from the crowd of underdog approval surrounding Alice.

Fortunately, the bizarre victory was short-lived. The next player struck out, and the teams switched positions. This time, Bree didn't need to go to Drew; he came to her, a dark crease forming between his eyebrows. He spoke with quiet irritation at the way his impressive run had been overlooked for Alice, without so much as a single clap when he scored. Bree nodded with approval to what he said next. Then, Drew jogged away from Bree and headed toward Alice, on his way to ask her to play third base. Now, surely, Alice's luck would run out.

Tyler was first up to kick, his face looking just as angered as Drew's. Somehow, Alice had managed to upset everyone who was used to being on top. And she liked to act like she was smart?

Drew pitched the ball to Tyler, who pivoted to the side as he kicked it, sending it over third base with intense speed. But Alice didn't hesitate, running backwards towards the edge of the field, keeping her focus up towards the sky.

A second later, Drew also began to sprint after the ball.

"Got it!" Alice yelled as the ball began to come down above her head.

Bree's breath caught in her chest. Certainly, Alice's luck had to run out!

It seemed Drew had the same thought, continued to barrel towards her.

Frozen in disbelief, the world kept moving around Bree. For the next six seconds, she existed in contradiction—stuck in place while everything around her sped up.

Second 1: The ball headed down toward Alice with severe force, but she clenched her grip with perfect timing, grasping it in her hands.

Second 2: Drew kept sprinting toward her, but Alice's eyes stayed fixed on the ball in her hands.

Second 3: Some students yelled at Alice to move, and others yelled at Drew to stop. One voice cascaded above the others, Jeremy's, it beginning to amplify as he started to run toward Alice, too.

Second 4: She realized how much closer she was to Alice than to Jeremy. She dug her toes into the ground, ready to head after Drew.

Second 4.5: Her body froze. She stood there, and she watched.

Second 5: Alice finally turned around, the look of triumph still on her face. She lifted her hand in anticipation, ready to wave to her teammates in victory—before she noticed how close Drew was to her.

In that same moment, the familiar image rushed back to Bree, and she pulled her hand, shaking lightly, up to her mouth. She no longer saw Alice standing there, but Emerson. Images of her sister's small, determined wave, sticking out through the car window every morning, with a genuine smile no matter how many times she was ignored, flooded Bree's thoughts.

In that second, Bree finally moved. She began to step toward Alice.

But it was too late.

Second 6: Drew's speed didn't come to a full stop; his arms shot out in front of him with just enough force that when they hit Alice's shoulders, she toppled backward and rolled twice down the hill toward the bottom of the fence, landing against her back in the slick mud.

There was no seventh second to act—only six, six paradoxical seconds that stretched out in slow motion yet flashed by like lightning. In those crucial moments, Bree remained frozen, but Jeremy was still sprinting toward Drew.

"Jeremy!" Bree yelled as he gusted past her. "What are you doing?"

He gave no indication that he heard her. When he reached the edge of the field, he grabbed Drew by the collar of his T-shirt and pulled him close.

"What is wrong with you?!" he shouted, shaking Drew in his fists.

Drew raised his hands defensively. "It's not my fault! I didn't think she'd catch it in time!"

"Well, she did, Drew!" Jeremy glared at him, a mixture of anger and disbelief on his face. "It was in her hands!"

"It… it just happened so fast!" Any defense Drew had drained from his expression, replaced by a quivering bottom lip. "I kept repeating to myself I would catch it, and then I… I can't remember where my thoughts landed after that." His face began to scrunch with fear.

Jeremy kept his fists on him but loosened his grip at the shift in Drew's demeanor. He glanced at the other students who had slowly made their way over. They all stood at the top of the hill, hesitant, as if they might topple over at any moment, too, while they stared down toward Alice.

Alice stayed planted where she was, as if the mud had glued her there. Only her arms moved, lifting toward the sky as she lay there. She stared at her dirtied palms for a long moment, then pushed them back down at her sides, finally sitting up.

When she did, her hair stuck out in every direction, solidified into strange clumps by the mud.

Alice began smearing her hands on her dress, frantically brushing them against the fabric in a repetitive, frantic motion, as if she were in a trance, ignoring the many eyes that were staring at her.

"Children! Children, what is happening?" The croaking voice of Mrs. Stitchley, as if her brain were lagging from her place on the bench, finally made its appearance.

The students parted as the teacher made her way toward the fence, gasping when she was close enough to peer down the small hill.

"Alice!" she cried. "What has happened?" She began to pick up her speed as best she could.

Alice didn't respond or give any indication she had heard her. She kept staring at her palms, turning red as she smeared the mud deeper into the fabric of her dress.

At the lack of response, Mrs. Stitchley turned toward the other students. "Well?" she raised her voice. "Someone tell me what has happened!" she demanded.

Bree twisted toward Jeremy, who now stood side by side with Drew, but they did not say anything. No one did.

But Mrs. Stitchley's focus was already back on Alice.

She bent her knees as low as they could go and began to head down the hill, her flats squishing into the soggy grass.

Finally, that prompted Alice to look up. She held a hand out in Mrs. Stitchley's direction.

"I'm fine, Mrs. Stitchley," Alice said. "I just fell."

It came out as a statement, firm in tone.

To Bree, it seemed this might be the first time Mrs. Stitchley was ever fully present on the field. The teacher seemed to breathe for the first time at Alice's response, her chest deflating as she stopped in her tracks.

"I'll go get the nurse! Hold on, hold on!" she said, backtracking and pivoting toward the school.

"Nobody move!" she ordered the other students as she walked quickly past them, in what appeared to be a nervous, frantic trance of her own.

Jeremy walked away from Drew, standing at the front of the students, but he didn't move down the hill. Bree hated the creases that formed on his face. She wanted to go to him and brush the lines away, but she knew her presence wouldn't do that.

However, she might have known the one thing that would let those lines soften.

Alice had stopped rubbing at her dress, now just sitting there like a statue in the mud, as if she was incapable of moving. Moving, truly, was so much harder than staying frozen.

But for Jeremy, Bree would make herself move.

Bree's feet sank into the wet grass as she headed down the hill, her knees bending beneath her so she didn't fall forward. She and Alice met eyes when Bree reached the bottom, and Bree bent over, reaching her right arm out toward her.

For one more moment, Alice stayed frozen. Then she reached out and grabbed her hand, the mud slick against her palm. Bree offered her a smile as she bent her elbow, bracing to pull Alice off the ground.

A small smile formed on Alice's mouth, too, but it didn't mirror Bree's. It was crooked in shape, tilting up toward one of her ears.

"Oh, and Bree," Alice said, squeezing her hand so tightly Bree could feel her heartbeat, "it looks like you fell too." She yanked her hand down toward her.

Bree's hands slipped on the wet grass as she dove toward the ground, her mind rapidly spiraling as she tried to comprehend what had just happened. Perhaps it was an awful dream she had fallen into, and any moment she would wake up. But the sounds around her began to seep further into her consciousness, rising in volume and hitting her eardrums like sharp pebbles. But the pebbles were her classmates, and the sharpness came from the backs of their throats, erupting in chaotic laughter.

She turned to look toward them, her face splattered with mud, wanting to scream at them to stop laughing at Alice, that there were clearly more pressing matters at hand! But as her eyes moved up toward the top of the hill, she realized their fingers didn't point and their stomachs didn't chortle toward Alice.

They were looking at her.

They were laughing at her.

They were standing there, while she sat here, below them.

Bree did not belong here. This was not her place, on this side of the judgment. She squeezed her eyes tightly shut and tried to tune them out, confused by how she could feel so lonely and exposed at the same time. She tried to focus on the only thing that mattered: the one responsible for all of this.

The same smile was still strewn across Alice's face, now curling into a more wicked shape as she looked at her. Bree would make her regret ever smiling at her! Without speaking a word, she took action.

Alice yelped as Bree lunged over her. Bree dug her hands into the mud and smeared it straight down Alice's cheek.

The chaotic shriek of students ricocheted off her ears, bouncing far away from any place close to her one she cared about.

"Get off of me!" Alice yelled as Bree felt two arms yank her upward. She dug her feet into the ground as she was pulled backward, kicking for leverage.

"Calm down, Bree!" Jeremy said, his voice warm against her ear. He pressed his forearms firmly against her stomach as he scrambled with her up the hill. She began to fight less against his pull, but she kept her vision firmly locked on Alice. Alice spat mud out of her mouth onto the ground, then dragged one hand slowly down her face, clearing the mud from her vision as casually as if it were water.

Then, Alice locked her eyes on Bree, staring. It wasn't a look of fear that lived behind them. It didn't even resemble anger. It was collected, her eyebrows stacked over her eyes, then her mouth, calmly.

Bree felt calmer with Jeremy's arms wrapped around her, but she could not help but feel it was not her he was saving, but Alice.

"Off, Jeremy!" It was an order, but she had regained her composure, her words coming out steady. He released his grip, keeping his hands hesitantly by her waist.

When his hands softened, Alice was up so quickly it was like she had levitated, taking calculated steps toward them both.

Bree felt the fabric pull around her waist as Jeremy tightened his grip once more, but she took a step away from him, gently pressing her hand to his chest. He didn't move back, but he let go as she put space between them.

Alice kept coming toward Bree, and Bree clenched her fists as they stared at one another, neither of them breaking eye contact.

Dauntingly quick, Alice grabbed Bree's wrist, but her grip was strangely delicate, making it easy for Bree to pull away if needed. Alice lifted herself toward Bree's ear.

"When do you think they're all going to notice, Bree?" Alice whispered.

Bree pulled her head away in confusion, but then Alice's grip finally tightened. She yanked herself back toward Bree's ear without hesitation.

"When do you think they're going to notice what a child you truly are?"

All Bree saw next was a black web, slithering across her vision. She reached her hand out into the dark space and felt the coarseness of one of Alice's muddy ringlets in her grasp. Then she pulled. Then she pulled as hard as she possibly could.

Finally, the calm composure Bree was used to from Alice broke. She yelped and dug her fingernails into the back of Bree's hand. Bree heard Jeremy shout her name a moment before she felt an arm wrap around her waist from behind her. At the same moment, Ruby called out a warning for Mrs. Stitchley's return, and Bree, reacting instinctively, untangled herself from Alice's head as Jeremy pulled her toward him. The circle of students crowding around them parted, the teacher, now accompanied by the nurse, looking down at the three students as they stood in a neat, little, quiet row.

Bree stepped away from Jeremy, hiding strands of detached blonde hair in her fists behind her back. Alice rubbed the top of her head with her fingers, her head tilted slightly to the side like she might topple over. Mrs. Stitchley looked like she might fall over, too, the shock clear on her face as she took in how much worse things had gotten in her absence. Alice didn't move toward Bree or try to grab her hidden hands to reveal what Bree had done. Instead, she spoke, addressing the two adults at the top of the hill.

"Oh!" Alice clutched her chest. "Bree was quite a hero! She tried to save me after I had fallen, but..." She turned toward Bree, sticking out her bottom lip with sadistic pity. "She ended up falling too!"

Jeremy placed a warning hand on Bree's back, as if he knew she was about to lunge at Alice again, but she only gritted her teeth, staying still and saying nothing to contradict Alice's version of events.

Perhaps, Bree thought, some of the students wanted to protect Alice. Most of the students certainly wanted to protect her. And still some, Bree figured, felt that speaking up was more of a chore than staying silent. No matter their reasons, not a single student said a thing.

A beat later, Alice clapped her hands with a little too much enthusiasm and headed toward Mrs. Stitchley and the school nurse.

Bree kept her eyes locked on the back of Alice's skull, which somehow still had a surplus of those stupid ringlets. She'd really been hoping to see a nice, shiny bald spot. Unfortunately, there was nothing to her liking, a head still covered with cheerful curls, so she shifted her gaze to her own feet, keeping her eyes glued there as she followed up the hill. She was careful not to get too close behind Alice.

TWENTY MINUTES LATER, Bree sat adjacent to Mary's desk with Alice sitting next to her. Bree stared down at her feet, which were swinging rapidly underneath her. The girls' parents had been called, notified that there had been an accident, but that no one was too badly injured. Alice and Bree were both being sent home for the day, to clean up from their... *accident.*

Now, Bree fixated on the glass window in front of her, waiting with an anticipation to go home that she might have never felt before. And then relief came—the silver car appeared on the road. Bree jumped from her seat. She did not look at Alice or Mary as she jolted towards the front doors, slamming her palms against the glass, bolting outside.

Once on the sidewalk, she lifted her hand into the air, looking for the back window to roll down and for her sister's small fingers to stick out their greeting. But they didn't. There was no big, enthusiastic smile, waiving from the backseat.

Of course, there wasn't. Emerson was in school. *Of course she is*, Bree repeated to herself. Her chest felt heavy for a moment, but then she decided to keep waving anyway. She waved big, above her head, her muddy hand hoisting itself into the air.

Victoria, when she pulled the car to a stop, waved back. She smiled endearingly, but with a slight look of shock— perhaps at her daughter's appearance, or her daughter's greeting.

Bree did not speak when she got in the car, her brain focused on only one thing. Victoria held onto her look of shock for a moment longer, but she, too, did not speak, pulling out of the circular driveway quickly. Bree unzipped her backpack immediately, pulling out her writing for Miss Tulip. The spacing was choppy, the lines uneven, the words repetitive and short. She crinkled it up immediately, knowing it would no longer do.

She would start again. She would put in as much effort as she did when she pumped her legs beneath her while running in the schoolyard. Control would be hers once again and not just in her field. She would take it to Miss Tulip's class, where Alice thought she had control. Bree would show her up at her own classroom games!

Tonight, she would practice reading out loud in front of the mirror. She would diligently watch the shape of her mouth as she spoke, feel the way her tongue hit the roof of her mouth as she formed her words, ensuring that each came out with confident precision.

It wouldn't just be her delivery that was impressive, but the content too. She wouldn't write about childish topics like grades, the way Alice had. Her piece would reflect *real* responsibility, adult-like responsibility. It would be the greatest address her classroom had ever heard. She would make sure of this, and she knew exactly how.

"Mom," Bree turned towards Victoria, "could you help me with an assignment when we're home?" she asked.

THE NEXT DAY, anticipation for the weekend radiated through Miss Tulip's classroom. As she read aloud from the textbook, the students' attention dwindled, their eyes drifting toward the door. Bree, however, teemed with a different energy. For the first time, she did not feel an eagerness to leave but to stay. All night, she had dreamt about the look of shock she would soon see on Alice's face. Bree wasn't sure how something like this could fill her with such exhilaration, but the feeling bubbled in her chest.

She squeezed her backpack against her thigh for the first forty minutes of class, worried that if she couldn't feel the rough fabric, it might disappear, her writing along with it. She glanced at the clock and watched it tick closer to what might have been one of the most important moments of her life. It would be a pivotal marker of what she was capable of, hopefully enough justification that she would never need to prove herself again. The last segment of class eventually came, with Miss Tulip's request for a volunteer rippling from the front, as perfectly calibrated as Bree's preparation.

Bree's fingers prickled as she shot her arm into the air.

All the students turned to look, but Bree glanced only at Alice, who had also turned, surprise etched across her small face.

Within this school, Bree had many moments in which to demonstrate her strength and capability, but soon, she would face her most important moment. She would rid her classmates of any doubts that had involuntarily woven into their minds about her because Bree was not just a leader in one area; she could take charge anywhere it was necessary. This was exactly what she had chosen to write about: leadership. She had chosen to discuss her leadership at home, showing that it was not just at school where people were drawn to follow her. At home, she had to be a leader for her sister, showing that good authority stands up and speaks for what they believe, as she would do now.

Bree's mind felt great clarity, and her body felt calm. Yet, a nervousness circled around her so strongly that it bounced to her heart, even though she was certain it was not radiating from herself. She tilted her head toward Jeremy, who stared down at his textbook, gazing at it bleakly, as if his pupils had sealed over themselves, unable to stir as excitedly across the page as they usually did. The only part of him acting in character was his knee, jittering in its usual manner. She tilted her head to the side, and exactly how she had expected, there was his paper pressed firmly against his thigh, the short sentences scattered down the page.

They had not spoken about English class, nor the happenings in the schoolyard yesterday. Spoken, yes, they had, but words were perhaps the thing on the planet that held the most potential; there were so many of them that it was easy for the difficult ones to float away, a strategy Bree employed expertly. But as she looked at him, she did not feel that she had the tools to know where to put these unspoken words, as they continued to build within her, pressing against her temples with their increasing weight.

The teacher called Bree's name, asking if she was ready, but as soon as she heard her name, a thought flickered behind her eyelids. It came without approval or permission but stayed firmly in place, repeating itself: perhaps this moment was not hers after all. Perhaps, to be the good leader that she was, she needed to know when to let others speak, too.

The students shuffled around her, putting their textbooks away and whispering to one another before they were hushed back down. Miss Tulip picked up a small cloth from beneath the dry-erase board, wiping in large, impatient swipes across the day's writing as she waited. Bree pressed her fingers against her backpack, but she let them sit there for a long moment, not unzipping it.

Then, she turned quickly, leaning close toward Jeremy, where no one else could hear.

"Jeremy!" she whispered, "I forgot my writing!"

He turned toward her quickly, and a flicker of a harsher emotion crossed his face, but he quickly masked it, keeping his kind, so-very-Jeremy voice on. He reassured her with a nod of his head. "Check again," he said. "It must be there."

"No! I'm certain!" she hissed, not looking back towards

her backpack. Bree's voice cracked, "I cannot tell this to the class! Not once I already volunteered!" She looked toward the front of the room hesitantly, then back to Jeremy, getting so close that their heads were an inch from one another.

"Jeremy," she pleaded, the sound of his name soft yet urgent, "you have to volunteer instead, so I don't need to tell them I forgot mine!"

Jeremy no longer masked the frustration, or perhaps panic, that etched into every corner of his expression. "Bree! No, I…"

"Jeremy!" she cut him off, letting her eyes grow as they met his. "Please." She held onto the word for as long as she could, making it as strong as six letters could be.

Miss Tulip's growing impatience was unmistakable as she called on Bree for the second time, her tone firm and insistent.

Bree shifted her focus hesitantly, turning back toward her backpack. She knew not only that Jeremy could do this, but that he would. She knew this so very well because the truth of the matter stuck out to her like a shiny piece of glass on the asphalt under her monkey bars. She knew he would do it because of a trait he held—to keep others on the top of the hill, as he himself would dive for the muddy pools of this earth. Bree believed she understood this more about Jeremy than he probably did himself. She knew the depth that would still be there once bits of his immaturity were chipped away. So she would be patient, and she would give him time. She would give him today. She would give him the space for silly jokes, pranks, and laughter, for a little bit longer.

Although she was most certain that he would speak up any moment now, as the sound of her backpack unzipping became the only noise growing in the silence, her confidence began to quiver. She opened the top of her backpack only slightly, her fingers tapping nervously at the zipper.

"Actually," Jeremy began.

Bree finally exhaled.

"Bree," Jeremy said, keeping his focus on Miss Tulip, "if you don't mind, I'd really like to read mine today." His voice shook slightly.

The stunned looks that turned toward him were even more surprised than when they had turned to Bree earlier, but the students did not say a word, and even Ruby silenced the chomping of her gum in that moment. Yet nothing in the room was as foreign as the expression on Alice's face—not the rigid, disciplined look she usually wore in class, but, if Bree had to name it, a sort of real smile.

Miss Tulip looked at Bree, who gave a casual shrug in response, nodding subtly toward Jeremy in what she hoped looked like detached approval. Inside, she could barely contain her excitement. In this moment, she had made him brave, but she kept her face still, pretending it didn't matter either way.

The teacher's lips pressed into an unreadable line, but then she nodded toward Jeremy and headed for her seat behind her desk.

"Okay... this is happening," Jeremy muttered, more to himself than anyone else.

He pulled the piece of paper from the darkness of his lap, standing and walking toward the front of the classroom. Bree kept her focus on him for a moment longer, ensuring that he was not going to turn back around and look at her. Then, she quietly slipped her fingers into her backpack, brushing them against the loose-leaf paper of her writing, tucked neatly at the top of her backpack, where she could easily pull it out. She zipped back up her backpack quickly, hiding her writing, as Jeremy turned to address the class. Then Jeremy cleared his throat, looking hesitantly towards Miss Tulip.

"I…" He cleared his throat once again, "Well, I didn't write this in the way you instructed us to. I hope that's okay."

Miss Tulip offered him a reassuring smile. "I'm sure the class will enjoy it, Jeremy," she said, leaning forward in her chair.

For a third time, he cleared his throat and began to read:

THE DINING ROOM **Table**

I want to describe what
home is.

IT'S A SHOTGUN HOUSE.

You can look all the way through it without ever needing to step inside.

The carpet is old. I used to like
the feeling of the dense ringlets against my hands.
The stains are more potent now.

· · ·

GHOSTS SIT under the dining room table. They are not dusted.

My mother likes to clean, but my father has asked her to, so

she doesn't. My hand hits their cobwebbed bodies, over and over,

with the jitter of my leg.

I DO CONSIDER SPOONING the soup into my ears.
But it drips
down my insides. It's too slippery.
My father likes thick soup.
My mother makes it loose.

AND THIS IS what you ask of me
to one day be.
And I did want it.
I wanted to grow,
Without knowing a thing about it.

JEREMY PAUSED FOR A MOMENT. Bree's body froze, but her mind spun around the "it" he had mentioned. *Could it have been?* Certainly not… Did Jeremy know the secret, too? Jeremy looked up toward the other students, but nobody moved. Then, after a long moment, Alice gave the slightest nod in his direction.

He looked back down and continued:

· · ·

I DO NOT WANT it anymore.

I do not wish to give away my childishness for respect.

I do not wish to give away my childishness for responsibility.

I do not wish to give away my childishness for you.

IT IS a shame that when I say this word,
childishness,
it takes a negative shape in your mind,
deformed and tangled in the undusted ghost's
cobwebbed chest.
But I think I'll keep the word anyway,
for I more rather be childish than sit in mature silence
around a very loud dining room table.
Bree was flabbergasted. He did know the secret! She wasn't sure how or who had told him. She thought she was the only child who knew. But it didn't matter. He was wrong either way. It would never work, this thing he hoped to stay—this belief that one could still be a child and be taken seriously. She had come to understand that, to be taken seriously, her thoughts needed to harden, shaping them into rigid forms that fit the mold of adulthood. Bree had already learned that the only way to earn respect was to grow up as fast as possible and forget childhood just as quickly. The faster she could reshape herself into something more structured, the more likely someone would be to listen to her, to think she had something meaningful to say, to care for her voice. That was the responsibility of becoming an adolescent, which Bree and her peers were now. She knew they were.

But either way, knowing this truth and knowing Jeremy was wrong did not stop her next action. When Alice began applauding, her eyes fixed on Jeremy, and the rest of the class followed. Bree could not help but clap in approval, too.

AROUND ELEVEN, the sound of an approaching rainstorm drilled against the school's roof. P.E. was held in the gym. Bree was not sure how long it would be that way, but it wasn't as boring as she anticipated it would be. It was actually *okay*. They played Four Square. Bree figured Mrs. Stitchley was trying to keep them as stationary as possible for the day, hoping that if they stayed in little squares, nobody would fall over.

Now, during pickup, the rain had hidden back among the clouds. Bree brushed her hand against the schoolyard fence, still stained a darker shade from the rain, as she walked up the sidewalk. She stood at her regular place, peeking down toward Jeremy as he was whisked away in his mother's dented car. They had still not spoken about any of the events yesterday, nor about him reading in class today, but perhaps, Bree thought, maybe such things did not always need to be discussed to be acknowledged. On Monday, she would smile at Jeremy, and if she was lucky, he would smile back, and that would be more than enough.

Bree turned quickly at the faint scuffle of something creeping up behind her. She wasn't in the mood for Drew's end-of-the-day snark. But it wasn't Drew leaning over his bike. It was, rather, a very small student, standing with what looked to be her strongest posture instead.

"So…" Alice held onto the word for a moment. "You just forgot your paper, huh?" she asked as if it were an accusation.

Bree's knuckles ached as she clenched her fists at her sides. Desperate as she was not to give Alice the satisfaction, she knew she couldn't admit what she had done in case Jeremy found out. It was now painfully clear that Alice didn't care that she wasn't supposed to talk to him. That hadn't stopped her before, and if she found this out, she'd be the first to skip over and tell him. Bree knew, in this moment, she had to put her pride aside.

For Jeremy, she reminded herself, replying, "Yes," through gritted teeth.

Alice's face did not morph into a smirk or a gloat of vindication. Instead, she kept her investigative, brow furrowed.

"Then let me see," she said.

"What?" Bree asked in confusion.

"Let me see inside your backpack." Alice took a step toward her.

"No!" Bree clung to the backpack against her chest defensively, squeezing it tighter as Alice moved closer.

Alice was an inch away from the backpack, but she halted quickly, her eyes locked on Bree's scared expression.

"Jeremy writes rather beautifully." Alice's eyes went wide for a moment, then she squinted them back at Bree. "You agree?" she asked, as if it weren't a question at all.

Bree nodded gently in response.

"But…" Alice went quiet for a moment. "I do think he

writes like a boy, not a man." She paused again. "I think it's rather brave to write that way, don't you?" This time, she didn't give Bree a moment to respond.

"Maybe you understand bravery," Alice said, glancing back at Bree's backpack, which was still clutched defensively in front of her chest. "Because what you did was…" She chewed on her cheek for a moment, then repeated herself. "What you did was rather fearless, Bree."

Then Alice turned back toward the school, walking toward the buses without another word, leaving Bree standing stiffly on the curb. Bree swallowed, her thoughts feeling too stuck to process. She was unsure how Jeremy always contemplated things for so long. It felt so uncomfortable. For the first time, maybe she did want someone to be able to reach into her mind and read her thoughts, so she didn't always have to try and make sense of them on her own. She wondered if they'd understand what was there, sitting in her brain with a little notepad, checking off boxes for the thoughts she should keep and the ones she should disregard.

Finally, with the stability she was used to, Bree heard her mother's car begin down the road. And now, she was not alone. Emerson's window rolled down, and Bree saw her pigtails dash out into the wind, her small face following. Her smile was bright as the breeze danced across her cheeks. Her hand appeared next, each finger like the growth of a flower bud, small at first, then opening with the eagerness of their greeting.

Bree slung her backpack over her shoulder, raised her hand, and waved toward the car.

. . .

ABOUT THE AUTHOR

Annie Lemerande is a recent graduate of Columbia College in Columbia, Missouri, with dual degrees in Psychology and English with a concentration in Creative Writing, along with minors in Women's Studies, Sociology, and Honors.

Her academic path reflected a deep interest in both analytical research and creative expression. During her senior year, she completed an honors thesis that combined psychology and literature, writing a 50-page creative nonfiction novella with a 20-page literary introduction that explored adolescence, identity, and the paradoxes of growing up. Currently, she is pursuing a master's degree at NYU Steinhardt in New York, continuing to explore the intersections of education, creativity, and development.